W9-CLL-845

The White Deer

AND OTHER STORIES TOLD BY THE LENAPE

By John Bierhorst

■

■

In the Trail of the Wind
American Indian Poems and Ritual Orations

Four Masterworks of American Indian Literature
Quetzalcoatl, The Ritual of Condolence, Cuceb, The Night Chant

The Red Swan *Myths and Tales of the American Indians*

Black Rainbow *Legends of the Incas and Myths of Ancient Peru*

A Cry from the Earth *Music of the North American Indians*

The Sacred Path *Spells, Prayers, and Power Songs of the American Indians*

The Hungry Woman *Myths and Legends of the Aztecs*

The Mythology of North America

Cantares Mexicanos *Songs of the Aztecs*

A Nahuatl-English Dictionary and Concordance
to the Cantares Mexicanos

The Naked Bear *Folktales of the Iroquois*

The Mythology of South America

The Mythology of Mexico and Central America

Lightning Inside You *and Other Native American Riddles*

History and Mythology of the Aztecs
The Codex Chimalpopoca

The Way of the Earth *Native America and the Environment*

The White Deer *and Other Stories Told by the Lenape*

Mythology of the Lenape *Guide and Texts* (forthcoming)

John Armstrong

THE WHITE DEER

and Other Stories Told by the Lenape

■

Edited by JOHN BIERHORST

■

WILLIAM MORROW AND COMPANY, INC. *New York*

Inquiries should be addressed to William Morrow and Company, Inc., 1350 Avenue of the Americas, New York, NY 10019.
Printed in the United States of America.
Designed by Jane Byers Bierhorst
2 4 6 8 10 9 7 5 3 1

Library of Congress Cataloging-in-Publication Data

The white deer and other stories told by the Lenape
edited by John Bierhorst
p. cm.
Includes bibliographical references and index.
ISBN 0-688-12900-5
1. Delaware Indians—Folklore. 2. Munsee Indians—Folklore.
3. Tales—United States. 4. Tales—Ontario. I. Bierhorst, John.
E99.D2W45 1995 94-30962 398.2'089973—dc20 CIP

Permission to transcribe from manuscripts and to reproduce photographs and other materials has been granted by the owners whose names appear in the picture captions and in the Notes and References in the back of this book. In a few cases, where owners or custodians could not be reached, appropriate identification and full credit have been given.

Frontispiece

JOHN ARMSTRONG / photographed between 1883 and 1887, died before 1904. Of Munsee Delaware and Seneca descent, Armstrong was a native speaker of both Munsee and Seneca and a principal keeper of Munsee tradition at the Cattaraugus Seneca Reservation in western New York. Recalling Armstrong and other native traditionalists at Cattaraugus, the anthropologist J. N. B. Hewitt has written: "They were men whose faith in the religion of their ancestors ennobled them with good will, manliness, and a desire to serve." (John Armstrong is the teller of "The White Deer," p. 67, and "The Twelve Little Women," p. 99. Photograph by Jeremiah Curtin, courtesy of the Smithsonian Institution.)

Acknowledgments

This book of Lenape stories would not have been possible without the generous cooperation of several individuals and institutions, namely, Haig Meshejian, whose deep knowledge of the Lenape was an initial source of inspiration; James A. Rementer, who provided unpublished texts and essential guidance; Bruce L. Pearson, who made texts available from his field notes; the National Museum of the American Indian, New York, which gave access to the M. R. Harrington papers; the American Philosophical Society, which answered numerous calls for research materials, especially from the Frank G. Speck collections; the Delaware Resource Center, Trailside Museum, Cross River, New York, which permitted the transcription of tapes in its keeping; and the National Anthropological Archives, Smithsonian Institution, Washington, D.C., which facilitated the study of the Truman Michelson and Curtin-Hewitt papers.

CONTENTS

Lost Children

Boy Heroes

The Trickster

Tales of Prophecy

Photographs

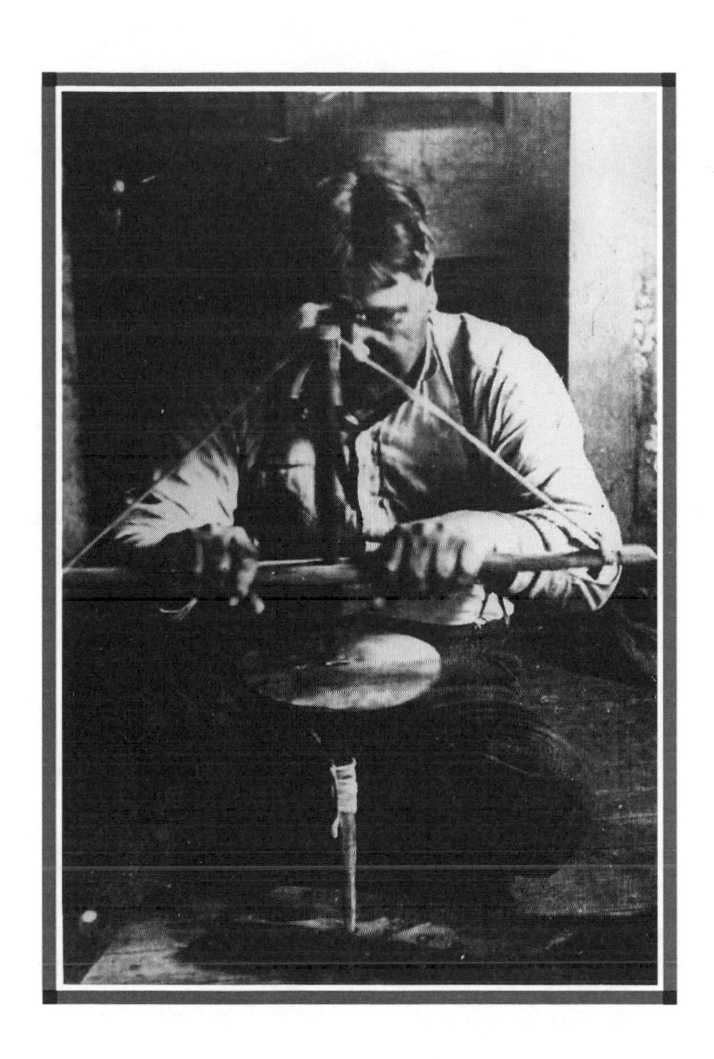

Julius Fouts

JULIUS FOUTS / 1862-1926, photographed 1909 or 1910. Called Pètanihing ("He Who Throws Something in This Direction"), Fouts—or Fox—was an Unami Delaware of Dewey, Oklahoma, and the husband of Minnie Fouts, another of the narrators represented in the present collection. He is shown with the fire drill, or "ringing noise-instrument," used to kindle the "pure" fire for the Big House ceremony. (Julius Fouts is the teller of "Ball Player," p. 56. Photograph by M. R. Harrington, former Glenn McCartlin Collection, courtesy of James Rementer.)

Introduction

The Lenape are the native people of New Jersey, southeastern New York, eastern Pennsylvania, and northern Delaware. The tribal name by which they have been known since colonial times—Delaware—comes from the Delaware River, where some of their ancestors once lived; and the people themselves, when speaking English, usually say they are Delawares. In their own language they are *lënape* (luh-NAH-pay), or, in the plural, *lënapeyòk*, meaning "ordinary people."

Those whose ancestors lived in New York and northern New Jersey are sometimes called Munsee Delawares, or Munsees. Their language is slightly different from that of the Unami, or Unami Delaware, once spoken in the southern New Jersey area. (The term *lënape*, as given above, is from the Unami; the Munsee form is *lënapew*, pronounced with a slight puckering of the lips at the end of the word.)

In this book the native name Lenape and the English name Delaware will be used interchangeably to mean either Munsee or Unami, or both.

The journey west

In the greater New York City and Philadelphia regions there are people today who can claim Lenape ancestry, and as recently as the 1950s a small group in Monmouth County, New Jersey, was able to maintain a tribal government. But for most Delaware-descended people in the East, the tribal heritage is only a faint memory. As early as the first quarter of the eighteenth century, the main body of Delawares, and with them their culture, began moving west.

Displaced by European settlers who were now occupying the old Lenape homeland, Delawares took up residence in western Pennsylvania and later in central Ohio. Eventually, broken treaties made it necessary for these groups to move again. By 1800 many of the people were settled in Indiana in the region of what is now the city of Muncie—a name that bears witness to the Delaware presence. By this time other Delawares had gone north to Ontario, and a small group had found its way to the Seneca territory south of Buffalo in western New York.

Obliged to move yet again, the Indiana Delawares in the 1820s pushed westward to Missouri, then Kansas. In Kansas they lost their lands once more, and in the 1860s they began moving to Oklahoma, where a smaller band of their tribe had already fled by way of Texas.

Today the principal Lenape communities are in southern Ontario, in eastern Oklahoma near Bartlesville, and in western Oklahoma near Anadarko. In Oklahoma the Unami language is still spoken by a few older people. The Munsee language is spoken by older people in Ontario.

Although it has been more than two hundred fifty years since the Delawares left their homeland, memories of the old country have persisted—especially in folk narratives. Storytellers often set their tales "in the East," or "at the mouth of the Delaware River," or at the Big River (the Delaware), or at the "other big river" (the Hudson).

In fact, some of the tellers whose tales appear in this book have been able to trace their personal ancestry either to New Jersey or to southeastern New York. One such teller was the late Nora Thompson Dean of Dewey, Oklahoma, just north of Bartlesville. Her family line goes back to a Kwëlpi̱kàmen ("He turns things around where he steps"), also called John Thompson, whose sister was a descendant of Tammekappei, known to Europeans as the Delaware "king" Salomo, born in 1672 near Cranbury, Middlesex County, New Jersey.

Another descendant whose ancestry can be traced was the late Josiah Montour of Six Nations Reserve near Cayuga, Ontario. Montour's grandmother, Shopsi, had taken her name from a place on the "big river," or Hudson, in New York State where her people had once lived. In English the word *shopsi* is usually written Sopus, or Esopus, an early name for Kingston, now the seat of Ulster County, New York.

In 1976, having traveled east for a visit, Nora Thompson Dean was asked by her host, "How do you feel about visiting the homelands of the Lenape?" Her answer: "I'm very happy to be able to come back here again, and I can understand why my people were very, very reluctant to leave this area. Where I live now, it's a flat country, and we're used to wooded area, hills. And it makes me happy to be back here to visit my old people's home *land*. Wherever I am, I always think that the spirits of my people are glad to see me. We believe in that."

When telling a folktale, Nora Thompson Dean would sometimes pay tribute to the old country by opening with the statement "Long ago when the Delawares lived in the East. . . ."

The written record

The proper way to preserve folktales is in the human memory. The telling itself, then, becomes an act of re-creation, a little different each time. Appreciating this tradition, Delawares in the twentieth century have continued to tell, or perform, the old stories, despite opportunities to write them down.

But if the stories are written, they form a permanent record. And this, too, has value. It enables people to look back and see what stories were told in the past and how they have changed—or remained the same.

When Europeans settled in Lenape country in the 1600s, they wanted to know how the native people had gotten there before them. Where had the Lenape ancestors come from? How had things begun? When the Europeans asked these questions, they were told origin myths. And the myths, sketchily jotted down by the newcomers in Dutch or English, are among the first Lenape stories on record. These myths tell how the North American continent was formed on the back of a turtle and how the ancestors of the Lenape grew up, or emerged, from the soil. In the early twentieth century such stories could still be told by Lenape people in Oklahoma and in Ontario.

Another of the old traditions is mentioned by the engineer Peter Lindeström, whose journal of 1654-56 from the colony of New Sweden (now the state of Delaware) tells of a hero who was born to a virgin. This mysterious man performed "many miracles," so Lindeström reports, then left the earth, promising to return. Possibly the reference is to the biblical Christ, of whom the Lenape had no doubt already heard. It might also refer to the native trickster-hero, Wehixamukes (way-he-kah-MOO-case), who fits the description almost as well. The information is too scanty, however, to permit a judgment.

Through the 1600s and 1700s occasional reports on Lenape folklore provide mere hints of what the whole tradition might have been. Somewhat more detailed are the scraps of folktales set down in the early 1820s by the ethnographer Charles Christopher Trowbridge, who mentions the "long story" about a "great" man named "Weekharmookhaas"—evidently the same as the modern Wehixamukes.

In the year 1883 the study of Delaware oral literature took a leap forward with the arrival of the folklorist Jeremiah Curtin at the Cattaraugus Seneca Reservation south of Buffalo. Curtin found Munsee Delawares living at Cattaraugus and was able to record folktales fully and carefully. Curtin's work at Cattaraugus was continued in the 1890s by J. N. B. Hewitt, who, like Curtin, preserved texts not only in English but in Delaware.

Between 1907 and 1912 two further collections, mostly from the Unami of Oklahoma, were made by the anthropologists M. R. Harrington and Truman Michelson. Though of considerable importance for the study of Lenape lore, the stories preserved by these two collectors have remained in manuscript at the National Museum of the American Indian in New York and at the Smithsonian Institution in Washington, D.C.

Additional collections from both Munsee and Unami groups were made by the anthropologist Frank G. Speck in the 1930s and 1940s. Of Mahican ancestry himself and already well acquainted with other eastern North American tribes, Speck made friends easily among the Delaware, with whom he kept in touch regularly.

In the 1960s, 1970s, and 1980s important collections continued to be made by the linguist-anthropologist Bruce L. Pearson and by the linguist James A. Rementer. Rementer had been adopted as a nephew by the Unami Delaware traditionalist Nora Thompson Dean and had become a member of the Delaware community. Dean herself, in collaboration with Pearson, Rementer, and others, recorded Delaware stories, some of which were published. Other stories, from the Anadarko area, were published (in the 1980s in two volumes) by the Delaware Tribe of Western Oklahoma.

Still further collections, gathered since the late 1960s, remain in the possession of scholars who have not yet made them available.

All in all, counting fragments set down by Lindeström and other early writers, roughly two hundred twenty traditional Delaware stories are now accessible. A close study of these texts has formed the basis for the selections in the present book, which attempts to display the variety of Lenape narrative tradition, while giving preference to versions that have not been published before.

A northeast tradition

As mentioned above, Lenape folk literature includes a creation myth in which the earth is formed on the back of a turtle. For the most part this story is remembered only in fragments. A typical example is the version taken down by M. R. Harrington about 1910, here given in full:

"The earth is flat and is supported beneath by a great mud turtle which carries the earth on his back. The muskrat began to build the earth in the first place when everything was water, on the top of a big mud turtle. And then the beavers came and carried more earth."

In addition—and much more fully told—are hero tales, star myths, animal stories, trickster stories (about the character Wehixamukes), and myths explaining how particular Lenape ceremonies got started.

Some of the stories are exclusively Lenape, not known to have been told by other Native American groups. Among such Lenape specialties are "Snow Boy" and "The Big Fish and the Sun."

"Snow Boy" tells of a strange child who bites other children's fingers, making them stiff as if frozen. When a little older, he departs on an icy stream, promising to return each winter in the form of snow, so that hunters can track game.

In "The Big Fish and the Sun" two boys travel to the sun's house in the sky, where they are given hot ashes to take back to earth. With these they boil an entire lake, killing a dangerous water monster.

A number of Lenape narrative types, however, are by no means unique. They are shared by once-neighboring or not-too-distant tribes, indicating that Lenape folklore belongs to the northeast region of North America—with a little spill-over into the southeast and midwest. Tribes that share four or more Lenape tale types (with the number of shared types in parentheses) are: Cherokee (four), Menominee (four), Ojibwa (five), Onondaga (eight), Seneca (fifteen), Shawnee (eight), and Wyandot (six).

Among the shared stories is a somewhat variable tale in which a bride is sought by a band of brothers. This tale type has been called "Mudjikeewis" (after the hero's name in Ojibwa) or "The Red Swan" (because in many versions the bride takes the form of a brilliant red bird). In the present collection the story is represented by a version called "Ball Player," in which the youngest of the brothers plays ball with a wildcat skull and the bride, mysteriously, has hair that is "shining green and blue."

Another of the northeast tales is "Bear Boy," the story of a child adopted by bears and later orphaned when his bear "mother" is shot by human hunters. In the best preserved of the Lenape variants his name is given as "Rock-shut-up"—appropriately, since the bears found him trapped in a hole beneath a boulder.

Still another is "Three Boys on a Vision Quest," with variants from the Menominee and Objibwa of the Great Lakes region as well as the Passamaquoddy, Maliseet, and Micmac of Maine and New Brunswick. This is a story about wishing, in which those who make reasonable requests are rewarded, while he whose wish is outrageous receives just punishment.

Less widely known—but reported from Cayuga, Micmac, Onondaga, Seneca, and Wyandot sources—is the humorous yarn about a man who misunderstands instructions and bungles every time. In Lenape versions he is part trickster and part folk hero. One of the tales emphasizing the trickster side of his personality tells how fellow members of his hunting party instructed him to go on ahead, find a water hole, and mix cornmeal—so the others would have something to eat when they caught up with him. But when they arrived, they found him uselessly mixing the meal *in* the water hole. According to one theory, his Delaware name, Wehixamukes, means "one who mixes." (Another source gives "one who repeatedly feeds.")

These and other stories show that Delaware folklore, even for those Delawares who now live in Oklahoma, retains a northeast flavor.

Many snows ago

Except for two texts collected as early as 1883, all the stories in this book were written down (or tape-recorded) between 1907 and 1984. During this period, opportunities to tell stories became fewer, and storytelling customs were less carefully observed.

But people still remembered the old rules, since these had been kept up, at least partially, or had been mentioned by parents and grandparents. As a result it is possible to say a few words about the manner in which stories were told in former days.

Generally, the time for telling was after dark and almost always during the coldest months. That stories must be told only in winter is a very old rule, widespread in native America. Delawares used to say that if tales were told out of season "the bugs would chase you" or "all the worms would take after you." Some said the ground had to be frozen; if it were not, and if stories were told, snakes and lizards would crawl into bed with you. As explained by others, there should be stories only "when things around cannot hear"—never in summer, when "everything is awake."

According to one source, if you do tell stories in summer you need to announce beforehand, "I'm sitting on twelve skunk skins." This is sufficient to ward off the harmful creatures, so they will not crawl all over you.

It is said, however, that there are two kinds of stories, real and fictional. The fictional tale, or (in the Unami language) *athiluhakàn*, is the one that must be told only in winter. Stories about real people or real events can be told anytime. This seems clear enough. But in practice it is not always so.

In the view of one knowledgeable traditionalist, tales about the trickster Wehixamukes are "winter stories." But another authority, equally knowledgeable, when asked point-blank if a Wehixamukes story is an *athiluhakàn*, replies cautiously, "Well now, wasn't there really a Wehixamukes?"

Often, stories that seem fictional are given a real setting by the teller, who connects the tale to actual places and historical events. Which stories, then, are fiction? And which are fact? To stay on the safe side, one can adopt the phrase used by one narrator who refers to winter tales as "stories which we do not know are true or not." Such stories—about which there is doubt—are better left untold during the summer months. (See the tale entitled "How the First Stories Came Out of the Earth.")

Usually stories are told by an older man or woman who has a reputation as a good narrator. In former times the narrator would keep a bag with an assortment of pebbles, corn kernels, and other small objects. These would be taken out one by one as the stories were related. When the bag was empty, the storytelling session was over.

While listening, people sat around in a circle and periodically answered the storyteller in chorus. Adding to the formality of the occasion, the teller would sometimes begin by using a set phrase, such as "Many snows ago . . . ," or "Long ago, it is said . . . ," or "My story camps. . . ." There were set endings as well. These might be quite simple, such as "That's the ending of that one" or "This is my story, an ancient one." Or, more elaborately, the teller might pick up a stick and snap it across his knee, saying—in the Unami Delaware language—*nkax*, "I break it off."

Originally, of course, the stories were told only in Delaware, and there are still people who can and do narrate in the native language. But by the twentieth century many storytellers were proficient in English and thus had become their own best translators. That is, they were able to re-create their stories in flavorful, idiomatic English. A number of these versions have been recorded—in what may be called spoken Delaware English—and several have been included in the present collection. "The Giant Squirrel," "The Big Fish and the Sun," and "Why Dogs Sniff Each Other" are typical examples.

Other stories have been preserved in what may be called literary Delaware English. In other words, the versions were not taken down by someone else but were written by the storytellers themselves, using a more formal English. An obvious example is "The Lost Boy."

More difficult to classify are some of the versions preserved by older anthropologists like M. R. Harrington and J. N. B. Hewitt, who seem to have taken down stories sometimes in spoken Delaware English and sometimes in English obtained from an interpreter, then rephrased. These include "Snow Boy" and "The Twelve Little Women."

Still other stories are preserved in versions dictated or taped in Delaware and later translated. Texts thus put into English by Frank Speck, C. F. Voegelin, Bruce Pearson, James Rementer, and Nora Thompson Dean are among those included here, notably "How the Big House Got Started" and "The Boy Who Became a Flock of Quail."

Since most of the stories in this book have come from manuscripts not previously published, some editing has been necessary in order to correct spelling errors and other minor slips. In addition, occasional nonstandard English verb forms have been regularized; and paragraphing has been established where there was none in the source.

Since many, if not most, of the versions were told for the benefit of people not thoroughly acquainted with Lenape culture, explanations are sometimes provided by the storyteller to aid the listener. For example, a narrator tells us there were "twelve *netyogwesûk*—little women." The explanation "little women" has not been added in the editing process. It is in the manuscript source.

In other cases the reader needs help but doesn't get it. What is a *manëtu*? The word appears mysteriously in a couple of the stories. It would have been easy to slip in a short explanation. But since there is none in the text, the reader will have to turn to the glossary in the back of the book.

The idea, in short, has been to stay connected to the story sources as nearly as possible, accepting their strengths as well as their occasional oddities, in the hope that the reader may thereby be brought closer to the Delaware tradition and may gain an appreciation of its long continuity, stretching back to Indiana and Ohio—and even to eastern New York and New Jersey, spoken of repeatedly by storytellers themselves as the places of the "dense woods" and the "great water."

ORIGINS

Nora Thompson Dean

NORA THOMPSON DEAN / 1907-1984.
Called Weènjipahkihëlèxkwe ("Touching Leaves"), Dean was one of the best-known Unami Delaware traditionalists of her generation. A resident of Dewey, Oklahoma, she became the teacher of anthropologists and a visiting lecturer at universities. Like her mother, she was gifted with visionary powers, which enabled her to serve as a name giver for her people. (Nora Thompson Dean is the teller of "The Giant Squirrel," p. 20, "How the Big House Got Started," p. 22, and the stories on pp. 82, 85, 111, 116, and 118. Photograph by Rae Russel.)

How the First Stories Came Out of the Earth

In the old days the Lenape had professional storytellers who went from place to place. People would gather around and offer tobacco or some other kind of payment in exchange for the stories about to be told. The little tale that follows explains how the custom got started.

A man returning from hunting found a curious hole in the ground. He looked into it and somebody spoke to him.

The hunter asked who it was.

But the thing did not tell him, only said it was a grandfather: "If anyone wishes to hear stories, let them come here and roll in a little tobacco or a bead, and I will tell them a story."

So the people came.

And that is the beginning of the stories which we do not know are true or not.

This grandfather told them never to tell stories after it begins to get warm in the spring. "If you do," he said, "the snakes, bugs, and all kinds of little creatures will get after you."

ANONYMOUS, *Oklahoma*

Snow Boy

There's an old Lenape story that tells how people once became cannibals when the snow was so deep they couldn't find anything but each other to eat. Other stories tell the good side of winter: for example, how corn magically appeared in an old stump during the cold months when people were starving. The story of Snow Boy is actually two tales in one. The first part tells the bad side—how winter sucks the life out of your fingers. The second part gives the good side—how the body of the snow person, spread out on the ground, helps hunters track game.

One time long ago a young girl had a baby boy. No one knew who was his father. They say he had no father.

When he was old enough to crawl around, he would get angry at the other children sometimes and when angry would take hold of their hands and suck their fingers.

It was seen that their fingers turned black and stiff as if frozen from cold when he had sucked them.

When he got a little older, he told the people that he could stay with his mother no longer, that he did not belong there, he must go. "My name is snow and ice," he said.

He said he had been sent by those above to show them how to track anything—people or animals. And he told them how to do it.

"When I come again," he said, "you can track anything: remember when snow falls that it is I who come to visit you."

Then he told his mother to take him down and put him on a piece of ice—to go down the river, for it was early spring.

They took him down and put him on a cake of floating ice. And beside him they put a bark vessel full of sweetened, pounded parched corn, *kahamakun*, for they thought he might need food. Then he drifted away down the river.

Until recent years the Delawares would go down

to the river with a little bark vessel of *kahamakun* as an offering to the snow boy. When a large piece of ice appeared, they would give two or three whoops, and the ice would swing in towards the shore.

Then they put the little bark boat on the ice and talk to Snow Boy. They tell him they are glad to see him again and tell him to take this corn with him. Then they ask him to help them in tracking game.

ANONYMOUS, *Oklahoma*

The Giant Squirrel

In native North America, tales about an ancient time when game animals hunted humans are told especially in the Pacific Northwest. In these stories, deer, beaver, and other harmless creatures are said to have once been larger or fiercer than they are today. To protect people, a mysterious Transformer changed the animals, taking away their harmful powers. And so, when the tables were turned, people ate animals just as animals had once eaten people. The Lenape are not known to have such tales—except for this one, in which the Creator plays the role of the Transformer.

Well, this is a story about a squirrel. At one time he was a very huge creature, and he went about the lands on the prairies—and the woods.

He killed everything he saw, and he would *eat* these different animals—the lynx, and the weasels, and wolves, everything he'd catch—he would eat these creatures.

And finally he saw a two-legged creature going along that he thought was another animal. So he caught this two-legged creature, and he killed him and started to eat him.

And the Creator saw him. And he came down to earth and he told him—he was sure scared, this squirrel, because he felt the power of the Creator—and he said, "Now then, you've done a terrible thing. You have killed one of my children. And from this day on, my children will eat you and your grandchildren and your great-grandchildren and all of your relatives, and you'll be small."

He'd consumed all of this human, except the hand. And when the Creator came he felt so scared and ashamed he tried to hide that hand under *here* [placing right hand under left upper arm]. But the Creator saw that.

And now up until this day, that hand is found on

the squirrel's ribs, where he had tried to *hide* this hand. And it's true, I guess, because I've dressed many squirrels, and there's a little hand right here, and we were told not to ever eat that. So I always cut it out.

[LISTENER INTERRUPTS:] "You mean there's a little piece of meat that looks like a hand?"

Um hm, little piece of meat, looks like a human hand—with five fingers. And that's what I was told.

NORA THOMPSON DEAN, *Oklahoma*

How the Big House Got Started

The Big House was the old-time Delaware church, a special longhouse where prayers to the Creator were offered during a period of twelve days each fall. Although the annual event (last held in 1924) included ceremonies that went back to pre-Columbian times, it is believed to have been given its modern form around the year 1800, when Delawares were living on the White River in Indiana. The following story gives one version of how this came about.

Before the whites came from across the water, the Delawares had a hard time making a living. But they were happy, because they could pray the way they wanted to, and they lived an enjoyable life.

At that time the Delawares and the Nanticokes lived near each other in the East, in Pennsylvania and in New Jersey. The Delawares were a little fearful of the Nanticokes, because they knew the Nanticokes practiced witchcraft.

After these two tribes had made a treaty with the whites, the whites betrayed the Indian people, saying, "This is our land. You must leave because we want this land."

Then the Delawares and the Nanticokes began to move west. They stopped at a big river, called White River, and began to build houses there. They made bark houses.

When they were watering their horses at the river, there was an old woman of the Nanticoke tribe whose horse carried a big bundle on its back. Also there were Delawares watering their horses.

Suddenly a Delaware man heard a baby crying inside the bundle on that old woman's horse. The old woman gave the bundle a whack and said, "Shut up! You'll eat soon enough."

It must have been a witch bundle, because several days later all the little babies got sick and finally died.

Then an old man said, "Tomorrow we will hold council. Soon we will know who the witches are."

The next morning they cut wood and used a fire drill to make a big fire. The old man sent for two men, and when they came he told them to go get the old woman, the one with the witch bundle.

Those two men dragged the old woman to the fire. Then the old man said to her, "Go get your witch medicine."

The old woman pleaded with them, saying she didn't have any witch medicine. Finally they burned her a little, and she said, "I hid it in the woods. I'll get it."

When she went after it, the two men followed her. The woman walked all around, saying, "It was here. It was here." Finally they grabbed her and started to take her back to the fire. Then she pulled the bundle out of a hollow tree.

Again they took the old woman to the fire, and the old man said to her, "Now throw the evil thing on the flames." But the woman refused. Again and again he told her. But she still refused.

Then they threw the old woman into the fire, and she burned up with her witch medicine. After that, they burned several other people, men and women.

Some of them must have been killed for nothing. All the people were in a strange state of mind.

All night long they sat up. The next morning it was cloudy. Thunder started, and there was rain. Then the ground began to shake. Everyone was afraid. People screamed, and they kept falling down. Everything blew away. Trees blew down.

Finally it stopped raining, and the earth was still. The wise men said, "We have done wrong. Our father, the Creator, must have been offended. We must all pray."

Then a few children were sent for—because the children were pure. The wise men thought, "Perhaps the Creator will accept prayers from the children rather than from the elders."

One old man went into the woods. He was gone a long time. When he came back, he looked happy. It seems he had received a vision. The old man said, "I met a strange-looking person wearing a bear skin and carrying a turtle rattle, and he held up his hand and said *ho . . . ho . . .* and began to sing." That strange-looking person must have been a *manëtu.*

The children listened to everything the old man said. They began to pray. While the boys and girls were praying, they started rising up into the air.

An old woman screamed, "Get some of those dirty clothes!" And they all started throwing the dirty clothes at the children. Several children were hit and fell back to earth.

But seven girls rose up and stayed permanently in the sky. Our old people used to say that these girls were the star cluster that can be seen in the fall.

When all this had taken place, the people made a longhouse with carved faces inside. Then every fall they prayed in this Big House for twelve nights. Our old people used to say that that's how the Big House got started. That's when it happened. My great-grandmother's mother was there.

NORA THOMPSON DEAN, *Oklahoma*

LOST CHILDREN

Josiah Montour

JOSIAH MONTOUR / born 1872, died after 1945. Called Xkokwsis ("Little Snake"), Montour was of Munsee Delaware and Mahican descent. In the photograph, taken in 1945 at Six Nations Reserve, Ontario, he is shown with Frank G. Speck (at right), whom he had helped in preparing materials for Speck's study of Munsee-Mahican ceremonialism, *The Celestial Bear Comes Down to Earth*. (Josiah Montour is the teller of "The Boy Who Became a Flock of Quail," p. 30, and the story on p. 79. Photograph by William N. Fenton, courtesy of the American Philosophical Society.)

The Sun and the Corn Bread

Delawares say the sun is "our brother." He lights the earth and makes food grow. But at noon he takes his payment by eating children—or so it used to be said nearly two hundred years ago. The story of the sun and the corn bread, told in the early twentieth century, shows that by this time the sun was no longer eating people in broad daylight. Instead, he was taking his payment by stealth during the night as he traveled from west to east.

One time in the night a man came in the house where there was a woman sitting and asked for something to eat. He wants her to give him some bread to eat.

She answered she had no bread or anything. Again he asked. But she said, "No, I have none."

"Yes," he said, "you have some bread." But she did not know it.

"Take some if you see it," she said, and the man reached over and picked up a loaf of corn bread from by her side. He cut it in four quarters, and every cut he made drew blood from the bread.

Then he ate that bread.

They say that man was the sun traveling back. And every child the woman had after that died right away. The sun had made his bread out of something that ought to have remained to give life to the children.

ANONYMOUS, *Ontario*

The Boy Who Became a Flock of Quail

Storytelling sessions used to include songs as well as stories. One kind of story, told as an entertainment for young children, serves mainly to introduce or explain the song that is contained within it. Several examples are known from the Unami Delawares. Here's one from the Munsees.

They say there was once a foolish woman, and she had a little boy. She left him by himself. When she came back he was nowhere.

She looked in the neighbors' cooking fire.

Then she found his tracks leading to a tree. He was singing:

pitiful
pitiful
all alone
it seems
I'll be a quail
*potchpai**

As he finished his song, one arm fell out of the tree. He sang again, and a leg fell down. Again, and his head fell. All of him fell. Each time, *potchpai.*

That's why the Delawares always hated to kill quail: they're that woman's little boy. It's why I tell the story. It's an ancient one.

JOSIAH MONTOUR, *Ontario*

*Call of the quail.

A number of the Delaware stories that have been preserved are examples not only of folklore but of literature. That is, they were written down by Delawares—often in English—with an eye toward careful composition. In this story about a boy who was thought to have drowned, it will be noticed that such phrases as "rushing speedily," "clairvoyant perhaps," and "mysterious deep" give the tale literary polish.

here was once upon a time three boys who were crossing a large stream. The stream was normally shallow. But when they entered, a great wave of water came rushing speedily down the river.

The boys, seeing their possible danger, hurried. But one of them was overtaken by the rushing water and was drowned, supposedly.

No more was seen of him. Which led to a search for his discovery, and it arose a great mystery as to whether he was dead or alive.

But he was not found.

This boy being the only child of his parents, some assistance was sought leading to his discovery, the parents learning that there was an aged man living near, who possessed some mysterious power, clairvoyant perhaps.

They went to consult the man concerning their son. This mysterious man was part-blood Shawnee and Delaware.

Upon learning the customs of the mystic man, the father of the missing boy had taken one gallon of good whiskey and one pound of chewing tobacco. And after an interview with the man, the father was told that he, the old man, would meditate. And in two days the father could come back, and he would tell him whether his son was alive or dead and where he was.

Upon the father's return, the aged man told him that he had taken the tobacco and one-half gallon of the whiskey into the forest and drank and smoked, and communicated with the spirits of the departed members of the tribe, and was told that their son was alive, had been taken by a woman to abide with her at the mouth of a great river.

Then on the evening of the second day, when the announcement was to be made to the tribe, the aged man told the father of the missing boy to announce that anyone wishing to see the mystery was to encamp on the bank of the great river opposite its mouth and that at sunrise they would see the missing boy.

Before the hour, a great crowd gathered at the appointed place, and the mysterious deep began to roll and throw forth great whirlpools. And thunder or rumbling sounds burst into the air.

At sunrise, behold, they saw on the waves of the great river the missing boy. At his side was a beautiful humanlike personage, said to be a mermaid.

No, this boy could not communicate with his parents. But, greatly to their satisfaction, they had seen their son.

Confidently knowing it was the departed son, they left the boy in the deep mysteries of the river.

Unto this day they do not know, but it is supposed, that he still remains there.

ANONYMOUS, *Oklahoma*

The Girl Who Joined the Thunders

There are many Lenape stories about spirits that cause thunder. One of the favorite types is the tale of a boy or girl who disappears from the earth to live with the thunder-beings. The young person who has been lost acquires a special voice heard by the people below—either a thunderclap that is louder or more high-pitched than usual or, as here, a continuous low rumbling.

One time there was a young girl who was very good-looking, yet years passed and she never married.

But at last a handsome young man, a stranger, began to come around and talk to her, and at last she began to like him, and finally she went away with him.

They traveled a long time until they came to a big lake. And here, to her surprise, the man went down into the water, and she was obliged to follow. But once she was beneath the water it did not trouble her at all, it was just like air.

Traveling on, a long way, they at length arrived at a little house where an old woman lived, who scolded the young man, saying, "I told you not to bring her here! She cannot live with us."

But the young man insisted. And they began to live together.

Every morning he would start out to hunt, and return in the evening with a deer on his back. And so things went, for a long time.

But one time the girl woke up at night thinking she saw a great snake in the house. Frightened, she ran out and away.

But the young man followed and caught her. "Why did you run away?" he asked.

"I saw a big snake in the house" was the answer.

"No. That was no snake," he told her. "That was only my clothes."

The same thing happened several times, until the girl made up her mind to escape.

And so, on her trips for firewood, she would wander away as far as possible, so as to learn the country in order to get away when the time came.

One day she started soon after the young man had set out for the day's hunt, and went a long way before she was discovered. But at last she heard a hissing, and a noise like a snake coming. And then the young man appeared.

She told him that she was merely going over to "that hill, to look around," and she went back with him.

The next time she tried it, when she began to hear the hissing noise of the snake coming, she thought of her dream helper, the weasel, and called upon him to save her.

The weasel ran into the snake's mouth and down into his body, where he cut out his heart.

So the girl was able to reach the shore of the water. And when she emerged, the Thunders were waiting for her and carried her up into the air. She never had realized, until then, that she had been underwater all this time.

When the Thunders took her up, they rubbed her body. And at every rub, many little snakes dropped from her into the water.

By and by, no more snakes dropped, and she was clean and human again.

The Thunders took her back to her home, and she told the people there what had happened, but she said that she could not stay with them but must live with the Thunders.

"I will tell you how you can tell when I am coming," she said. "When a cloud comes up making a continual rolling or rumbling sound, that is the noise made by my garments."

ANONYMOUS, *Oklahoma?*

Rock-shut-up

Tales of lost children adopted by bears are among the oldest of Lenape stories. Similar tales are known from the Seneca, Penobscot, and other tribes of the Northeast. In this version the hero—who is usually known simply as "the boy"—is given the name Rock-shut-up, or "he who has been closed in with a rock." As it happens, there was an Oklahoma Lenape man born 1837, died before 1898, who was actually called Rock-shut-up. Possibly the name was taken from the story. Or perhaps the story, set down about 1910, was told in memory of this man.

One time long ago there was a fellow going out hunting with his wife and a little boy, his nephew. After they got a ways, the woman decides she does not like this boy, because it is not hers or her man's, although it is his nephew.

When they eat, they give the boy the skimmings from the soup and nothing else.

After a while, the woman hated the boy.

And finally the man took the boy away from the camp to where there was a hole in the ground, not far from where they camped. He told the boy, a little bit of a boy, "You go into that hole as far as you can go, into the ground."

So the boy went in there, and this man picked up the biggest rock he can carry and set it upon the hole so the boy can't get out.

And he went back to the camp and left the boy there.

Not very long after that, the animals found there was a boy shut up in that hole.

The buffalo tried to push the rock to one side so that the boy can get out. But he could not move the rock.

A bear came along and told the buffalo, "I can take that rock away with just one hand." So the bear threw the rock away from that hole.

The boy in there was pretty near starved.

The buffalo told the bear, "You are the only one who could take care of him and raise him up."

The bear took the boy to a she-bear who had young ones. The boy thought they were children and never knew the difference—where they lived, in a hollow tree, the boy never knew any difference—he thought they were his folks sure enough.

■ ■ ■

In the fall of the year, all these bears went out pecan hunting, and while they were picking them up—there would be a lot of old ones in a bunch—they heard some hounds and someone whooping, following the dogs.

So the bears ran, every one towards their home, and this human boy and a girl bear and a boy bear ran to their tree and ran into the hole. The mother bear had told the kid they were his brother and sister. There they lived. Finally the boy was pretty good-sized.

One time, when they were running into their house, they saw a little light at the door. And this mother bear went up and licked that light off, and went back to her bed again.

She looked up again, and there is that little light again at the door. She went up and licked it off again and told the young ones, "They will not find us now."

In the fall again, they went out pecan hunting again. The bear brother says, "Let's play a trick on these old fellows. When they have a lot of pecans, let's go way off from the crowd." They did this. And the bear said, "I'll bark like a dog and you can whoop."

So they did that.

All the bears who had been pecan hunting ran to their holes where they lived, and the boys went back to the place where they had been gathering the pecans.

When they got there, they found big piles of pecans, which the big bears had gathered. They took all they could carry, up to where they lived. And when they got there, the mother asked them, "Did you hear those dogs barking?"

The boys said, "Yes. We did that to get the pecans these old grandpas had gathered and give them a scare."

She said, "You go and tell those grandpas that you did it, so they can get their pecans. And take these back where you got them."

The boys did that.

And finally they went out pecan hunting again, and they got all they wanted and went to where they lived.

When they got home, the old mother saw the light again on the door.

She went and licked it off and went back to bed.

But when she looked up again, there was another light which she jumped up and licked off. She did that from morning until noon.

She told the young ones, "They will find us now. I can't rub that light off that door."

She said the man who was to find them wore owl feathers on his head. So she told the boy, "When they call us 'Come out,' I want you to get out first. Take your little bow and arrow and stick that out with your hand first, so they won't kill us. If you don't do that, they'll sure kill us."

That afternoon, that man came up there and knocked on that tree, and said, "There are bears in there." So he made a whoop.

So the people began coming from every direction. He said, "There are two or three bears in here."

And they got up there and told them to get out.

The mother bear told the boy, "Now, go out, so they won't kill us. You go first." But nobody wants to get out.

And they heard them say outside, they are going to build a fire and throw some down that hole. And the mother bear told the boy, "Get out! They will throw fire in here. Hold your bow and arrow first." But he would not go.

So they threw fire in there, and the mother bear got out, but she said, "They will sure kill me."

Then she got out, and they shot and killed her.

The other boy, the bear, got out. And they shot him.

Then there were only the sister bear and the boy.

She said, "I am not going out. They can burn us up in here, but I am not going."

So they threw more fire in, and the sister bear put it out. But she said, "I am not going to put it out anymore. You must go now." And the boy got out.

He took his bow and arrow and stuck them out the hole first, before he came himself.

When he got out, they told him to get off the tree, which he did. They told him, "We never would have killed the others if you had come out first."

They asked him if there was another in there. He said, "Yes, my sister is back in there." So they called her out.

She got out. And they made her get off the tree.

Before she did so, one fellow got tobacco and tied it on this young bear's neck. They talked to her, and told her, "We would never have killed your mother if the boy had got out first."

And they took the boy with them.

When they got home where he used to live, he knew his uncle's name.

He now had the power to kill any game, for he knew where they stayed. These bears called the boy *a'sun-kê-pon'*, "Rock-shut-up." That was his name.

ANONYMOUS, *Oklahoma*

BOY HEROES

Minnie Fouts and Warren Longbone

Minnie Fouts / photographed 1909, died 1945. Called Wèmeehëlèxkwe ("Reverberates Everywhere"), Fouts was a resident of Dewey, Oklahoma, and the wife of Julius Fouts. Well known for her beadwork, ribbonwork, and other traditional crafts, she helped plan the attempted revival of the Big House in 1944. The second photograph, taken in the early 1930s, shows her grandson, Warren "Judge" Longbone, playing the game of ring and pin. (Minnie Fouts and Warren Longbone are the tellers of "Three Boys on a Vision Quest," p. 75. Photograph of Fouts by M. R. Harrington, courtesy of the National Museum of the American Indian, Smithsonian Institution, neg. 2897; photograph of Longbone, from the former Glenn MacCartlin Collection, courtesy of James Rementer.)

The Big Fish and the Sun

In one of the best known of all Lenape stories, two heroes face a peculiar monster for which there is no completely satisfactory English name. The creature grows to enormous size. It lives in water and has the upper body of a human and the lower body of a fish. When telling the tale in English, storytellers sometimes say the thing is a "mermaid" or a "merman." Here it is simply called the "big fish."

There was an old woman who had a granddaughter six or seven years old who became pregnant. No one knew how, for in those days children were pretty well guarded, not as today.

When the old lady kept watching the girl when

the child was born, thinking it might be born at any time, when the girl took sick to deliver the child, when it came, it was a little fish.

So the grandmother when she saw it said, "Is this my grandchild?"

It was a little fish she was looking at. So she didn't know what to do, for it was a water animal and she didn't know how to take care of it. So she picked it up and remembered a swampy place. Over there.

When she got there, she saw a little pocket of water, where some livestock had tramped there.

She put that fish in the water. The little fish swam round and round in a circle.

Next morning she went back there to see her grandchild the fish.

When she got there she saw a big lake there, and this fish had already grown to be a large, good-sized fish. It was still swimming round in a circle, as when she'd first turned it loose.

■ ■ ■

That lake grew to an enormous size. And this fish, the last time it was seen, was an awfully large fish.

The mother of the fish went over there one day, but she didn't see it, the water was so deep.

They began to find out some people would go in

that direction and would never come back. So they didn't know whether it was this fish who killed the people or not.

They didn't know for sure. They got to watching it because everyone who went in that direction never returned.

Finally they found out for certain it was that fish who got the people.

■ ■ ■

So the chiefs got together after they found out this fish was killing the people.

So they counseled together to find out a way to kill that fish, because it was going to do worse if it was not done away with some way.

They decided that among the tribe there was probably someone who could kill it.

So the people gathered this wampum. That was the money those days. They got a big abundance of it. So they took those beads to the chief.

They told the chief those beads were to be given to whoever said, "I can kill that fish," or whoever said, "I know a *way* that fish can be killed."

So the conjurers began to gather where the beads were, as the people all decided they knew no other way of getting rid of that fish.

Well, there was an old woman very poor who lived on the outskirts of the town. She had two grandchildren, boys, who stayed in the bark house all the time eating parched corn. The old woman went every day to where they were counseling.

Well, one day one of the children asked the old woman why she was always going over to the town.

She took up a club and hit him over the head. "Why do you inquire about other people's business? There's a big pond over there, it grows larger and larger. And there's a large fish that grows larger and larger. It will soon eat up the whole tribe if it is not killed."

"Well," said the boy, "I can kill it."

So the old lady, knowing they were looking for someone to do this, next morning went up to where the big gathering was. So she told the people there what this boy had said.

So then the *puchël*, a man elected to carry messages, was notified to come to the big gathering. When he got there, this *puchël* was told, "So get those little boys and bring them here"—for the reason that those little boys told their grandmother they could kill this fish.

So when the *puchël* got to where those boys were, he told them what he came for, that he had come to get them. So those little boys, who were writhing in the dust in front of the fireplace, jumped right up and went with this *puchël*.

So when the *puchël* got them to where the chief was, the chief asked those little boys, "Well, my grandchildren, I understand you can kill the fish over here in the big lake."

So the little boys said, "Yes, that's what we said we could do."

So the chief told them, "My little grandchildren, that's why we've been gathering here, for the purpose of finding someone who can kill that big fish. There's the big pile of beads, wampum beads. If you boys kill that fish, you'll get all of those beads right there."

So after the chief told them, they went back home and their grandmother went with them.

When night came, they did nothing, just sat around the fireplace. So the old lady wondered how in the world the boys were going to kill that fish. She got to watching them.

■ ■ ■

So bedtime came and those little fellows made the pallet pretty close to the fireplace.

So they lay down the usual way, kind of talked awhile.

The old lady didn't want to go to sleep. She wanted to watch these boys. She didn't go to bed.

Finally she went to bed, she lay in bed awake, she was going to find out about the boys. She was watching them but didn't want them to know.

So these little boys lay in their bed as if they were asleep, silent.

So when she went to sleep, the boys heard her snoring. The younger one said, "How are we going to proceed, to kill that fish? He's an extra-large fish and doing great damage."

The older told him, "Well, I don't know any other way but this: the Sun is my friend, so we'll go up and get his fire," the big boy said.

The young brother told the older brother: "Now how will we do, to get to where the Sun is?" It was after dark, you know.

So one of these boys, the older one, turned into a raven. The younger one turned into a pigeon.

So the older boy said, "That's the best I can prepare you. *You* cannot turn into a raven, you can turn into a pigeon. But I will help you, as I can, get to where the Sun is."

So he said, "The Sun lives in a house far across the big water. He goes there every night before he gets up in the morning. You, being a pigeon, cannot get there. You will fall. But I, being a raven, can help you. Every time you fall, I will fly under you and raise you. That way we gradually can get to where the Sun is."

So when they got to where the Sun's home is, they went into his house. The Sun hadn't got there yet.

And there was an old lady there who was the Sun's grandmother. They asked her if the Sun was there. The grandmother said he had not yet come, but would be in, in a short time.

So when the Sun began to appear at his house, he came in with flashes of light, into the house. The older brother had hidden his little brother in the corner, back of the door.

So the Sun saw the boy anyhow, even if he was hidden. So the Sun told the older boy, "Who is that?" The older said, "That's our younger brother."

So the Sun asked the older boy what they came for. "Well, we came to get your fire."

And the Sun asked what he wanted with the fire. The boy told him, "We want to use it to kill a big fish that's doing us big damage."

So the Sun said, "No, you cannot use my fire, for the reason you will burn up the earth that you live in. But you can go to my ash pile"—off quite a distance, these ashes had been a good many years back.

So those two boys got the ashes, tied them up in very small bundles.

So. Those two boys went back with the ashes.

■ ■ ■

When they got back there, they went to this big lake, to watch the fish's movements.

So. By the way this fish moved when they got there, the fish seemed to know what their intentions were when they got to that lake: it was by this fish being so powerful and knowing things ahead.

So these boys counseled together and turned into several different things in order to get next to this fish.

So. They found out he was going to be kind of hard to handle.

They used little insects to approach him. They found a pale butterfly. They sent him to the fish to locate him. The fish paid no attention to the butterfly, didn't watch him, or anything.

So the boys decided the butterfly was the very one needed by them to get near him. So one of these boys turned into this kind of a butterfly, as they found out the fish didn't watch it or pay attention to it.

This butterfly got pretty well on top of the water

flying around. The other boy dove down in the lake to the center of the earth, and he turned the ashes loose there which he had brought from the Sun. And this other boy, the butterfly, turned his ashes loose into the water.

So then they left and went home. And when they got there, they lay down on the same old pallet. The night wasn't over.

■ ■ ■

Next morning the old lady woke up and looked over and saw those boys there, asleep.

So the old lady picked up a wooden poker and began beating the boys. "Here you are asleep. And you said you were going to kill that big fish."

So the older boy said, "Go out and look at the lake and see what we've done."

So the old woman went there, walking around, and saw no water in the lake—she went on walking toward the lake, she didn't believe those boys, when she got to the lake she saw no water.

She saw that great big fish lying from one end of the lake to the other, burnt to charcoal.

So the ashes which the boys used, which they had got from the Sun, were so hot they'd dried out the lake and burnt the fish into charcoal.

The old lady after she found out how the fish was

killed, went and told the tribe about it. So they all went over there and looked at the fish that was killed.

So they gave the beads to the older boy for a reward, for killing this fish.

After they gave him the beads, those two finally grew to be men and were looked upon by the tribe as being something very great.

So when they grew up, the older one came to be a chief in his band, was well thought of, got to be a great man, powerful.

CHARLES ELKHAIR, *Oklahoma*

Ball Player

The adventures of a hero often make for a long story, and the tale of the young hero named Ball Player is among the longest on record. There used to be plenty of time to tell such tales, however, because in the old days—going back some two hundred years—Delaware storytelling sessions lasted all night. Even in more recent times the sessions would go on for five or six hours, beginning at about nine in the evening. People lay around the fire and relaxed—but no one was expected to go to sleep.

Once upon a time there was a family. Old man, and old lady. Told the boys, "We ought to go out and camp where there is plenty of game to kill." So they went.

When they came so far, they camped where there was plenty of game and the boys soon went out to hunt, for game. And the old lady made shelves to put the meat in. There were six of the boys.

And the youngest one never went hunting. He played with his ball whenever they went out hunting.

In the morning the youngest boy would go out with his ball and play all day. Sometimes he would go east. His ball was a skull of a bobcat. Whenever he would throw it, it would stick on a tree—if he hit. The skull seems to bite the tree and stick there.

They stayed there a long time and went hunting every day, they had lots of meat, and the old lady told her boys never to go hunting very far west. The oldest boy thought, "I will go hunting west."

When he traveled far out west, he saw a lake. And saw a young lady sitting on top of the water combing her hair. Her hair floated all around her.

He just could see her, then she disappeared. From there he went straight home. He liked her looks very much.

He never killed anything that day. When he came home, he thought, "I will try and get that girl tomorrow." But he never told his mother.

When it was daylight, he started off to the west, to where he'd seen this young girl when he came close to the lake. And he said, "Whirlwind, my friend!"

And he broke a stem of grass and he went into it and told Whirlwind: "My friend, I want you to help me get that girl." And when he'd done this, a wind started to whirl, and the whirlwind took the stem of grass right to where the girl was sitting.

And he couldn't get hold of her but one hair from her head. And he took it home. And when he got there, he put it on the backside of the bed.

When he came home, his mother told him, "I guess you have seen that girl."

Meanwhile, the youngest boy kept playing ball. Every time he would hit a tree, it would bite it.

■ ■ ■

Next morning the girl came and brought lots of bread, and the oldest boy married her.

She was a pretty girl. Her hair was shining green and blue.

She came to the bed and picked up the one hair

that had been taken from her and put it back in her head.

She told him she wasn't supposed to get married, for a certain fellow couldn't leave her alone, the fellow wanted her, and she told her husband to watch for him, that man's name was Red-Feather-on-the-Head.

And the boys went hunting again, with their brother married.

And this youngest boy grew to be bigger every day. And would play with his ball, and come late in the evening.

The oldest boy told the youngest boy to play around close to the house and watch his sister-in-law, and see that nobody takes her away. The youngest boy played with his ball close to the house.

And finally he went off and stayed all day. The youngest boy's name was Ball Player.

They had lots of meat. And had plenty, and never wanted anything. And one morning the old folks told the young people that they were all tired of living, and they went out where it was marshy and the old lady sat down and said, "You can always think of me when you see this": and there stood a weed instead of the old lady.

And the old man sat beside her, and *he* turned to a weed.

And these young people lived here by themselves and had plenty of meat of all kinds.

■ ■ ■

One morning, when the boys went out hunting, the man came who is called Red-Feather-on-the-Head. Came to the house, and the woman was alone.

The man took the woman and took her home.

The woman pulled up trees on her way to Red-Feather-on-the-Head's house.

And when they came home from hunting—and it was a long time before Ball Player came home—next morning the oldest boy told his brothers, "I am going to follow the woman," and picked up his flute and blew it, and said, "If they kill me, in two days blood will come out of my flute."

In two days the boys looked at the flute, and they saw blood on it.

And the *other* older boy said, "I will follow where our brother went." And he blew the flute and hung it up and said, "If they kill me, blood will come out of the flute."

In two days they looked at the flute. And saw blood, coming out of the flute.

But Ball Player kept on playing with his ball, every day.

So the next older boy said, "I am going to follow our brothers," and blew the flute and said, "If they kill me, in two days blood will come out of the flute."

In two days the boys looked at the flute and saw blood.

And the *next* older boy said, "I will follow my brothers," and picked up the flute and blew it and said, "If they kill me, in two days blood will come out of the flute."

In two days the two remaining boys looked at the flute and saw blood in it.

But Ball Player kept on playing ball, every day. And he wanted his brother to let him go. He said, "I can bring our sister-in-law back."

But he told him that hc was too little.

Next morning, the next-to-smallest brother took the flute and blew it and said, "If they kill me, in two days you will see blood come out of the flute."

When the next-to-smallest brother came to where Red-Feather-on-the-Head lived, Red-Feather-on-the-Head said, "What did you come for?"

He said, "I am looking for my brothers who came over this way, and my sister-in-law."

"Yes sir," said Red-Feather-on-the-Head. He told the women to "cook for the man who is very tired and hungry, he must've come from a long ways."

The women went to work cooking. They broke up bear ribs and cooked them and put them into a dish and gave it to Red-Feather-on-the-Head, and he started to give it to him.

And he started to take it.

Red-Feather-on-the-Head jerked it back: "You think that I am going to give it to you? I am going to feed it to my *yakwahe*." He turned him loose and fed it to him and said, "Yakwahe, eat this! And crush this man's skull in, when you get through. He has been talking about your sister-in-law!"

When he got through, he told the *yakwahe* to kill the rascal, and he went to the young man and soon killed him and took him down in the ditch.

■ ■ ■

In two days Ball Player looked at the flute and saw blood.

And he went out to a branch, where they got water. He whooped and called all of his friends around him. And he took his father's otter-skin tobacco pouch.

When he whooped, all of his friends were with

him. And he told the toad, "What can you do to help me?" The toad commenced to breathe. And whenever he would breathe, fire would come out of his mouth.

Ball Player said, "That is good enough. You can be my pipe."

And then Ball Player took the snake and said, "You shall be my pipe stem."

And he took the otter tobacco pouch and shook it and said, "What can you do to help me?" The otter said, "I can eat on his spinal cord and break him down."

He said, "That is good enough!" Ball Player said to the weasel, "What can you do to help me?"

"I can go down his throat and cut his heart off while he is fighting."

Ball Player said, "That is enough!" When he'd got enough to help him, he went up on the hill and made a fire, and made six arrows. And every time he made one, he would throw it in the fire. And when it would burn to ashes, he would pick the ashes up and rub them between his hands and throw a good arrow out on the ground.

And he did the arrows that way for ten times each, and took his ball. And he had everything with him.

And he took the same trail, for he could go by trees which were pulled up along the road—which the woman had pulled up.

■ ■ ■

When he came to where Red-Feather-on-the-Head lived, he walked in. And Red-Feather-on-the-Head asked him, "What did you come for?"

Ball Player said, "I am looking for my brothers."

Red-Feather-on-the-Head said, "I threw some ornery little boys out here in the ditch, maybe they are your brothers. My *yakwahe* killed them."

Then he said, "Cook for him, women! Maybe he is hungry, he's come from a long distance."

The women went to work and cooked some bear ribs, and Ball Player took his pipe out, and tobacco pouch. And started to smoke. Whenever he would draw the pipe, it would say, "We will kill him!"

Red-Feather-on-the-Head said, "Gee, your pipe sounds bad."

Ball Player said, "That is natural for my pipe to sound." And the weasel came out of Ball Player's pocket and climbed all over him in a second.

And Red-Feather-on-the-Head saw it, and he said, "You have a pretty little pet! We will fight our pets. Mine can crush your pet's head off in a little while!"

Ball Player said, "All right! My pet never was whipped." And by this time the women had the ribs cooked.

He wanted to give Ball Player the dish. But Ball Player said, "I don't want anything to eat. I came to hunt my brothers."

So Red-Feather-on-the-Head gave it to Yakwahe and told him when he got through to crush the weasel's head. "He is talking about your sister-in-law!" he said.

The women all were glad, because they thought he would kill Red-Feather-on-the-Head.

Red-Feather-on-the-Head was a fellow with one eye and had a red feather which he wore on his head. When Yakwahe got through eating, Red-Feather-on-the-Head told him to crush the weasel's head, and they went to fighting.

When the *yakwahe* opened his mouth, the weasel disappeared, and the otter commenced to eat his hind legs off, and broke him down.

Every time the otter got a mouthful, he would go and puke it out, and go after him again. And finally the *yakwahe* had to sit down to fight.

And the little toad got in front of the *yakwahe* and commenced to throw fire out of his mouth, so as to weaken him.

And Red-Feather-on-the-Head said, "Take them off! They will kill my pet."

Ball Player said, "No, let them kill one another."

In a minute the weasel came out of his mouth and brought out the heart of Yakwahe. And then Yakwahe fell, and he killed him.

Ball Player told his pets to go after Red-Feather-on-the-Head. And Ball Player threw his ball at Red-Feather-on-the-Head and hit him on the eye that he could see out of.

And the ball stuck there and Red-Feather-on-the-Head could not take it off.

He couldn't fight because the ball was in his eye. They killed him in a few minutes. They cut Red-Feather-on-the-Head's head off.

The women were glad that he killed him. But they said, "You haven't killed him yet."

■ ■ ■

Ball Player went outdoors and built a fire. The women helped all they could. They went and got wood to build the fire.

Ball Player threw Red-Feather-on-the-Head and Yakwahe into the fire.

They burned awhile. And then Red-Feather-on-the-Head's head popped: it went to the north. And the weasel soon brought it back.

It popped four times, and the weasel got it every time.

And next time it popped, it fell about the edge of the grass. They threw it back again into the fire, and then it couldn't pop anymore.

The women said, "You have killed him now."

The women all wanted to go with Ball Player. But he wouldn't go with them, only his sister-in-law.

And from there they went to where his brothers were lying. He stretched his bow and took one arrow and shot the arrow up in the air and said, "Look out, I might hit you!" And when the arrow hit the ground, the oldest one jumped up.

And he did the rest of his brothers the same way and they all went back home to where they lived—and took his sister-in-law with him.

This is the end of this story.

JULIUS FOUTS, *Oklahoma*

The White Deer

In Lenape lore the white deer is what has sometimes been called a master of game. It controls the other deer, who are thought to flock around it or follow it. Game masters can be helpful, because they have the power to give game to hunters. But they can also be dangerous, since they need to protect their charges from humans who hunt too often—especially humans with a child at home who needs to be fed. Here, then, is a story in which a young hero's parents are said to have been killed by the game master—who later becomes helpful to the boy himself.

An old man lived in a forest all alone except for an infant wrapped up in skins. All his relatives and all his nation had been carried off.

He placed the child on the other side of the fire, till after a time he saw it move. Then he said, "Perhaps the little fellow will live." The child had been left to him.

He made some thin soup of deer's meat and gave it to the little boy. He grew very fast. And the old man made him a bow and arrows.

After a time he asked where his father and mother were, if they hadn't any neighbors. The old man wouldn't tell him.

He waited awhile and asked again. The old man said he had had parents and friends but they were killed, would tell him no more.

The third time he asked, the old man said, "They have all gone in the direction of the Great Game, *ganyo gowa.*"

But he wouldn't tell in what direction that was.

One day the little boy started off thinking he would look for the Great Game.

He came to a small lake, and in the lake was a beautiful swan.

He aimed at the swan and killed it, then he didn't know how to get it as he had no canoe. So he made a line of bark, attached a stone and a hook, and threw it beyond where the swan was, and drew it in, a very large swan.

He shook the swan till it was small. Then, taking it on his back, he started home.

When near home, he struck the swan till it was big as before. Then he said, "Grandfather, I have got the Great Game."

"Oh," said the grandfather, "you shouldn't have killed that swan. That is a harmless bird. You take him right back to the lake and bring him to life again."

The boy took back the swan, put it in the water, pushed it off, and said, "You go off and amuse yourself and live in the water." The swan swam off alive.

■ ■ ■

After going back home, the boy again insisted upon knowing where his parents were, until his grandfather told him that he must go off to the east, that it was a six years' journey for an ordinary man. But a man of power could go there very soon. Halfway was a wizard spring, in which an ugly creature lived. And there his parents and all his friends had perished. He must be careful.

The boy set out, and before noon was at the spring.

When he came to it, he was very thirsty. The water was clear and seemed refreshing. He thought he would drink, but first he would put his foot in the water and see what would happen.

Drawing off one of his moccasins, he put his foot in the water, and the instant he touched it a terrible creature pulled his leg off from the hip and devoured it.

Now he had but one leg. "Well," he thought, "I'll try again, see if he will pull the other leg off," and he pulled off his other moccasin. The moment he touched the water his other leg was pulled off.

Now, being without legs, he sat down, pulled hair out of his head, and braided a fishing line, saying, "I'll see if I can catch this creature," and putting a wooden hook on the line, cut off bits of his flesh and put them on for bait and dropped the hook into the spring.

It was swallowed immediately, and he jerked a strange creature onto the bank. It was hairy, something like a man and still like an animal.

It began to cry piteously, "Oh, grandson, put me in again."

He let the hook down a second time and caught a second creature, a female, which cried like the first, "Oh, grandson, put me in again."

"Oh," said he, "I can do nothing without my legs. Vomit up my legs."

The male vomited up one leg, and then the female vomited up the other. They pushed them towards him.

He spat on his legs, put them to his body, and was as well as ever.

Straightening, he gathered a great quantity of dry wood, and set fire to it, saying, "I can't put you in again. You have destroyed all my friends."

He burned them up and went on. As their heads burst, great swarms of mosquitoes came out.

■ ■ ■

Then he traveled on till he came to an old house in an opening. On the top of the house sat two great white horned owls. When they saw the boy, they called out to someone below: "Wake up, old man. Somebody is coming."

The boy sprang into the house. There sat an old gray-haired man. Sleeping in his bosom was a white deer.

As soon as the boy entered, the deer left the old man and, coming to the boy, went into his bosom. The boy turned to go home, and as he went, all the animals of the world, and all the birds, followed him.

When he reached the woods, the old man woke up and, finding he was alone, said, "I think my brother must have another grandson, who has stolen my white deer." He started off with his club, overtook the boy, and called, "Why did you take my white deer?"

"What do you want of him? You are an old man. I am young. It is more useful for me."

The old man sprang for the boy, pounded his head flat, and, leaving him for dead, returned home with the white deer—sat down in his house and slept, with the deer in his bosom.

After a time the boy recovered. Putting his hand to his head, he found it was all flattened out. With both hands he brought his head to its former shape and turned back toward the house.

As soon as he entered, the white deer left the old man again and entered the boy's bosom. Again he turned homeward, all the birds and animals following.

When he reached the edge of the woods, the old

man rose up again and said, "I'll kill you," and he pursued him.

The boy now turned upon him and beat him to death with his club. He continued his way home unharmed, carrying the white deer in his bosom, and all the animals of the world followed him.

■ ■ ■

He reached home and told his grandfather of all his adventures, how he had come to the house where the old man slept with the white deer in his bosom, how he took the deer and the old man pursued him and beat his head, how a second time he had taken the white deer, fled and was pursued, and when the old man came up he killed him.

The grandfather asked him to describe the old man. When he heard the description, he began to cry and say, "Why did you kill my brother?"

That night when the boy was asleep, the old man stuck three arrows in his back.

On waking up in the morning, his back was very stiff and sore, and he said, "Oh, my grandfather has been trying to kill me."

He pulled out the arrows and in great anger said to his grandfather, "You tried to kill me and now I'll leave you here alone."

So he started off in the early morning for the west, taking the white deer and all the game of the world that runs and flies. The old man was left in loneliness.

■ ■ ■

He traveled on, till he came to a house in an opening. Then he took the deer out of his bosom and put it in a hollow tree. He went on to the house, where he found a boy of his own age.

"Where do you come from?" asked the strange boy.

"From the far east."

"Oh, that is the land of the *ganyo gowa*, who commands all the animals."

"Oh yes, I have the *ganyo gowa* myself," said the boy.

"Can you kill any kind of game you want?"

"Yes."

"Can you kill raccoons?"

"Yes."

"Could we go and kill some now?"

"Yes."

The two young men went on till they came to a very large tree covered with raccoon scratches. They climbed up and killed many raccoons, carried them home and made themselves a blanket.

The young man of the east thought he would always live with the young boy. So he went to the hollow tree, took out the white deer, and told him to go wherever he wished, he was free. And from that time, animals roamed the world at will.

JOHN ARMSTRONG, *New York*

Three Boys on a Vision Quest

Like European fables, Lenape stories may include a moral—or what is sometimes called a "correction." The story that follows is unusual because it includes not one but two "corrections."

There were once three Lenape boys who were sent on a vision quest. A *manëtu* came to them and asked what they would like to be when they grew up.

One boy said that he would like to be a hunter. Another said he would like to be a warrior. The last one said he wanted all the women to like him.

When they grew up, that came to pass. The one boy was a fine hunter. The other was a good warrior.

But the third one, who wanted all the women to like him, was killed by a bunch of women at a gathering who ganged him and tore him to pieces. He should only have asked for one woman to like him.

There are two morals to this story: One is to not be greedy when you ask for something, and the other is to not ask to be more than you can be.

WARREN LONGBONE as told to him
by Minnie Fouts, *Oklahoma*

THE TRICKSTER

Willie Longbone

Willie Longbone / 1868-1946. Called Pwèthìkàmën ("He Who Pushes Something in This Direction"), Longbone was one of the principal traditionalists of the Lenape community in the area of Bartlesville and Dewey, Oklahoma. A singer in the Big House, he was also an accomplished narrator. In the late 1930s he provided the information for C. F. Voeglin's studies on Unami Delaware language. In the photograph he is shown with his wife, Annie Wilson Longbone, called Kixkwe. (Willie Longbone is the teller of "Crazy Jack," p. 81. Photograph courtesy of James Rementer.)

Jack Babysits

The Delaware character sometimes called Jack, or Crazy Jack, is among the silliest and most outrageous of Native American tricksters. Many of the stories about him, like this one, make him appear worthless, at best. But the storyteller is not to blame. Notice that he begins by saying, "my story camps," indicating that the tale has a life of its own and has merely decided to "camp" here for a while before traveling to another location.

My story camps, called by name Jack.

Jack nursed the baby when all had gone away. While nursing, he had been told, he must drive away the flies.

Well, this Jack got angry at the flies and said, "Just wait a little and I'll kill you." He went and got an ax.

When he came back, the flies were flying on the child's face. He raised the ax, and as hard as he could he hit the flies on the little child's face—he killed the child.

Then Jack was scared. "Now what shall I do?" he thought to himself. "Here's what I'll do, I'll kill the goose and wear its feathers. I'll just be sitting when they all come back."

This Jack had killed the child, this Jack was scared. Then he went and sat where the goose had been sitting on eggs.

The woman's little boy and all the other people said, "Where could this Jack be?" They found him under the house where the goose should have been. Crawling toward him they saw him, this Jack. He was sitting there.

He made a loud noise like a goose sitting on eggs. Just like a goose: *ssssss,* it sounded. And there were Jack's buttocks sticking out of the feathers. *Ihí!*

Jack was a small person, though yet a man.

JOSIAH MONTOUR, *Ontario*

Crazy Jack Puts His Nose to the Ground

In Delaware tradition the trickster is best known for his habit of misunderstanding what people say, then doing the wrong thing and either bungling horribly or simply making a fool of himself—and here once again, as in the previous tale, he exposes his bottom.

He set off with the hunters. When they'd gone a little distance, the headman said, "Over there! You people go that way, over to that brush." And the ones that were to go had to flush out the bears.

Then the headman said, "You people here, put your noses to the ground!" He said to Crazy Jack, "Here, you! Put your nose to the ground."

"All right. I can do it," he said.

Now the ones that had gone to the brush scared the bears from the other side.

Immediately Crazy Jack dug a hole in the ground, putting his nose into it as far as he could. When the others came around—look at this!—somebody's buttocks sticking out.

The headman asked him, "Did you see any bears?"

"No."

He still had his nose in the hole.

"That's not what I told you to do," said the headman.

"*Flu!*" he said. "You should have told me what you really meant."

WILLIE LONGBONE, *Oklahoma*

Wehixamukes Story

Although the trickster can be called Jack, he is more often known by his Delaware name, Wehixamukes, pronounced approximately way-he-kah-MOO-case. In the following story we begin to understand that there is more to Wehixamukes than mere foolishness.

Long ago, supposedly, there was a person called Wehixamukes. When he talked, he talked incorrectly, and it seemed that he didn't have good sense. But Wehixamukes was powerful, and he was wise. He always acted that way because he wanted to fool people and he wanted to test them to see how they'd treat him.

One time he went along when several men set out on a hunting trip. They said to him, "You must cook and cut wood and clean everything up."

"Right! That's it!" said Wehixamukes.

When the hunters left camp, Wehixamukes picked up an ax and went into the forest to cut kindling. While he was cutting wood, he accidentally hit himself. He began to scream, "Help! Help!" He forgot he was all alone, because he had acted silly for so long that at last he was that way permanently.

When the others came back from hunting, they saw him all stretched out in the hut. "What are you doing?" they asked.

"I hit myself by accident," said Wehixamukes. "My hand hurts." "Tie some bark on your hand," said the headman.

The headman also said, "I'm hungry! I could eat a turkey dipped in grease!"

Wehixamukes heard everything the headman said, because the next morning they couldn't find him and finally one man saw him up in a tree, and his hand was tied to the trunk.

"Get down! Get down!" said the headman. "That's not it. I meant for you to first cut the bark from the tree."

"You should have told me," said Wehixamukes.

Then, that evening when the men came back from cutting wood, they saw Wehixamukes dipping a turkey in a bucket—and it had the feathers on, and the innards were still inside it.

"What are you doing?" they cried.

"Yesterday I heard you say, 'I wish I could eat turkey dipped in grease,' " said Wehixamukes.

Once again they told him, "That's not it. First, pluck the turkey. And you have to take out all those innards and cook it, and *then* you dip it in grease."

"You should have told me," said Wehixamukes.

■ ■ ■

Wehixamukes and the other men stayed home for several days because they were afraid of wild tribes.

Finally Wehixamukes said, "Let's go hunting. I'll go, too, and I'll kill all those wild tribes."

The other men exchanged glances. They were thinking, "Bungler." But anyway, they let him go hunting with them.

Before long, they lost him.

One of the men said, "We'd better watch out. Seems like wild tribes around here."

Finally they heard Wehixamukes giving the war cry, a big yell. "Here we are! Here we are!" he cried.

The headman called him down, told him, "Now then, you'll have to go knock out those wild tribes, now that you've let them know where we are."

"You should have told me," said Wehixamukes. Then he went and killed all those wild tribes.

This is just one story. There are many different Wehixamukes stories. That's all I can tell.

NORA THOMPSON DEAN, *Oklahoma*

More Wehixamukes

The trickster is a complex figure. He may be foolish and mean. Yet he cares deeply for his people. Here is a Wehixamukes story told by one of the most knowledgeable of Lenape traditionalists, who, on a different occasion, explained that the so-called trickster is also "our folk hero."

Here again is a Wehixamukes story.

Many long days ago, when the Lenape lived in the East, in the faraway land of Pennsylvania, they must have been numerous, and there must have been many different tribes at that time. A person had to be always on the lookout.

And it must have been difficult to live, to find food, because there were no stores the way there are now in our lifetime. Everybody used animals. That's what they lived on.

People had to hunt all the time and kill deer and fish and fur-bearing animals. They used the skins of the animals for clothing, grease bags, moccasins, and all the different things that they made.

The Lenape men camped in different places, beside rivers and in forests. Everybody went hunting. They needed to find food.

One time when these Lenape men went out to hunt, Wehixamukes went with them.

Walking in the woods, they came close to a prairie. Suddenly the headman stopped. He pointed to the north and said, "Wild tribes over there! We'll keep ourselves hidden. Maybe they won't see us."

Wehixamukes said, "Wait, let me play a trick on those wild tribes."

Then Wehixamukes set off running. When he got to some woods, he stopped. He saw where a deer had been killed. Things were strewn all over the place—head, antlers, a bladder. And blood all around.

Wehixamukes picked up the bladder and put it on his head. Then he set off running again.

He lay down in the road. But first he smeared the blood on his face and neck and hid his war club under his clothes. Then he laid himself down. He thought, "Those wild tribes are just about to come."

Must have been true, because when he opened one eye, he saw those wild tribes all coming along in a bunch.

When the wild tribes got close, they all stood around looking at Wehixamukes. One of them kicked him.

Wehixamukes held his breath. He didn't move. They thought he'd been scalped. "Must be a dead man."

Another one kicked him. But Wehixamukes didn't move a bit.

Then when they all turned around and were about to go, Wehixamukes stood up and whipped out his war club and started hitting them on the head. He killed them all. Not one was left.

When he'd finished, he gave the war cry. Then he ran back to where the other men were. He was panting, and he looked weak. One of the men said to him, "Surely you have great power, and you must be strong."

Wehixamukes answered. "Yes, friend," he said.

"For a long time I have known that I am strong and powerful. It is because the spirits gave me their own strength and power. And I will tell you all now: I feel that soon my life will end, but I will come again when the whites treat you badly. You will know me because I will be born with a finger missing from one of my hands. And a young woman who is a virgin will be my mother."

The men were surprised when they heard what Wehixamukes said, because for a long time they had known him to act silly, and talk silly. Then they all went home together.

When they got to where they lived, they cooked deer meat and corn mush—and deer tongue, because Wehixamukes liked to eat deer tongue. Those men were trying to treat him well, for they were still amazed at the way he had talked. When they had all finished eating, they went to sleep.

Next morning they all set out. They cut wood and they were chopping down trees. And when one of the men cut down a tree and it fell, it crushed Wehixamukes, and he disappeared in the earth. Immediately they tried to dig him up. But they couldn't. It was too late.

The men left for home. When they got to where

they lived, not one of them said a word. No one could eat. They filled their pipes, and they smoked. They were sad. The men now missed Wehixamukes. But there was nothing they could do. It was too late.

That is all I can say of what was told to me by my late mother. It has been a long time since I've heard our old people say, "We will wait for Wehixamukes."

NORA THOMPSON DEAN, *Oklahoma*

Six Stories About Wehixamukes

Trickster tales are often told one after another in what may be called a "cycle," or a trickster "epic." Here are six such tales, all told by the same narrator on the same occasion.

[He oversleeps]

Wehixamukes when he was grown was very ornery. He was dirty, lay down anywhere, and had no get-up to him.

A bunch of Delawares went out looking for enemies, so he wanted to go along. They hardly liked to take him, as they didn't think he amounted to anything, didn't care to be bothered with him.

They took him along.

And where they camped, he slept so long, the next morning they just left him there. So when he woke up, his men had all left him.

So he caught up with the gang of men where they were camped. When he got there he just lay down by the fire and went to sleep.

Next morning they woke up, ate their breakfast. And they left him, then again just let him sleep. They said, "Just let him stay there."

He knew all about it beforehand and was well satisfied.

So then he caught up with them again—he got up early.

[He alerts the enemy]

Then they went on, and they struck a big prairie country.

While going along, they ran into a big body of men that it was impossible for them to whip. So the headman said, "We'll now have to hide in the high grass so they'll pass us and we can go on." So Wehixamukes, just as *he* acted, squatted down as much as he could.

Every now and then he would stick his head out. "Look out, the people will see you," he was told.

So he couldn't stand it when the enemy passed him a bit. He jumped up and beat his breast, crying out, "Here we are, we're a big body of men." [NARRATOR ASIDE:] There were only thirty or forty in the bunch, and four or five thousand enemies.

[He defeats the enemy single-handedly]

So after he did that, the others with him jumped up and told him he'd have to throw down all the enemy, since he had got them started.

So then he said, "All right," and threw his blanket away.

[NARRATOR ASIDE:] He *understood* them to say, "Grab them and throw them down but don't kill them."

So he grabbed one and then another and laid them down.

So the chief told him, "That isn't what I told you to do. I told you to kill all of them because they're going to kill all of us."

And Wehixamukes said, "Why in the world didn't you say so in the first place."

And he grabbed his little ax and went right after them.

[He finds a "bear" hole]

After he had done this, he and the others went on. They struck a timbered country.

They were hungry and were without anything to eat. So the chief made remarks to the crowd that they all ought to hunt bear so they would have something to eat. "Now we'll scatter out and look for a nice hole." [NARRATOR ASIDE:] That's liable to be a bear hole.

"If any of you find anything, you must whoop, and we'll all go to it."

So they all started out.

Directly they heard Wehixamukes hollering far off somewhere.

So he discovered a hole on a big stem of grass, and a bird had cut that hole, and lived there.

So when they got there, he said, "Here's a hole. It looks as if someone was living in there."

"My goodness, no bear can go in there!"

"Why, you ought to have told me so in the first place," he said.

[He hunts "everything alive"]

Some said: "We'll go on a hunt and kill everything alive that we see and take it home with us." So Wehixamukes said, "All right."

While he was hunting, he saw one of his companions ahead. He thought, "Well, he's alive, I believe I'll get him."

So he killed him. He cut holes in his legs so he could carry him on his back.

When he went on farther, he saw another one of his companions. So he did the same to him, strung him up, went on home looking for anything that was alive.

When he got home, he threw the two men down in front of the people. "Well, this is all I could find alive."

[NARRATOR ASIDE:] The instructions were to kill anything alive.

So the old man said, "Now the thing's happened just as I told you he'd do. So now he's played this trick on us, he's killed two men. I always told you that you should explain everything fully to him, so he would understand it right."

So the chiefs notified their bands that they had discovered that he had such power he could do anything.

The chiefs told the bands hereafter to be very particular in talking to him, that when they tell him anything, they must explain it fully and kindly so he would understand it right.

[He sinks into the earth]

He had a sister-in-law living. She went off down to the creek and started to chop down a tree.

At the time it was ready to fall, Wehixamukes walked up just where it was going to fall, so this woman saw him just as he got even with the tree. She said, "Wehixamukes, you are so powerful and can do anything, let's see you catch this tree as it falls."

He said, "Oh yes, I can catch it," and he threw his hands up.

So she chopped the tree so it fell right on him.

He held the tree up, but he sank into the earth clear up to his knees—but kept the tree from the ground.

He kept on sinking till he sank into the ground till he sank to his neck, so the last word he told his sister-in-law was: "So! I guess I will have to leave you all. I will be back when the big general war on this earth comes off."

He said that whenever a little girl had a baby with the little finger cut off at the joint, that boy would be him, and there would be a general war.

When he finished talking he sank into the ground.

But he was still alive.

It was as if someone were going some place.

Silas Longbone, *Oklahoma*

TALES OF PROPHECY

Martha Ellis

MARTHA ELLIS / 1900-1982. Of Delaware and Shawnee descent, Ellis was a distinguished member of the western Oklahoma Delaware community of Anadarko. A speaker of Unami Delaware, she also spoke Caddo, Wichita, and one of the Apache languages. (Ellis is the teller of "Why the World Doesn't End," p. 106. Photograph by James Rementer.)

The Twelve Little Women

The Lenape have a tradition that a certain prophet among their ancestors predicted the arrival of the outsiders who in the early 1600s began settling in Lenape country. Here, however, is an unusual story in which the coming of the Europeans, or "white-eyed people," is foretold by twelve supernatural little women.

In the cliffs at the mouth of the Delaware River, on the right bank, were four openings in the rocks leading to the house of twelve *netyogwesûk*—little women. People used to bring articles of value and leave them for safekeeping in these caves.

When any man passed by sailing on the river,

these women would come out and ask where he came from, where he was headed, and how everything was growing.

If they received a kind answer, they let the passerby go on with good wishes. They were satisfied.

If he was impudent in his answers, they immediately ran down and chased him.

If they caught him, they plucked out every hair on his body except the hair of his head.

If they were unable to catch him, they called on their uncle, a great serpent, who lived in a deep hole in the ocean outside the mouth of the Delaware River.

Their uncle would come immediately, raise his head above the water, and draw a breath that would sweep the man into his mouth.

All the older and better people gave kind answers to these women, but younger and thoughtless men were sometimes insolent.

■ ■ ■

One day a young man, when asked where he was going, said, "I won't tell you."

That moment they rushed down after him, chased him, caught him, left no hair on him but the hair of his head, and sent him home bleeding.

He went to the chief and complained, saying,

"Why have we such women? Let us drive them away. Let them go to some other nation."

"Oh, never mind," replied the chief. "They don't hurt good people. Let them stay where they are."

So matters went on. All right-minded persons gave them kind answers, had good luck, and went their way undisturbed, while evil-minded ones were plucked, or swallowed by the serpent.

The little women made bags of the hair which they took from men, and with these bags the twelve women went out to the waters where fish were caught.

They asked of each fisherman something to put in their bags, and no matter how many fish the man had in his canoe, their bags were never full.

If the fisherman gave his fish willingly, he caught so many afterwards that he didn't know what to do with them. If he grumbled, he caught no more, had bad luck.

When the twelve women went home and emptied their bags, the fish—which, on going in, had become so small that thousands of them would fill a little bag—gained their natural size again.

■ ■ ■

One time a number of young men were insolent to the *netyogwesûk* and went home all bleeding from the loss of their hair. They complained, and all the young men said, "We must get rid of these women. They cause too much trouble."

Just then, one of their number said, "I can put an end to them."

So next day he passed by the caves and was insolent to the women. They chased him all over the flats opposite their house. Couldn't catch him.

Then they called on their uncle, who rose up that moment out of the water and began to draw in his breath.

The young man then made up his mind to be swallowed by the serpent. So he yielded to the current and went into the great open mouth.

Inside the serpent it was like a great room, his ribs like planks in a house.

The man cut a ridge along one rib, then another—with a flint knife—penetrating to the skin.

The serpent immediately rushed into the river, and above the river raised himself high in the air and landed on the flats opposite, once to the west and struck with all his power on the sand, once to the northwest and struck on the sand, then once to the north. In this way he made three channels.

The young man now cut his way out and, running to the southwest, went around to the rear of the women's dwelling.

When they saw the serpent's trouble, the women began to cry and weep, saying, "Our uncle is dying! Our uncle is dying!"

They hurried down to where he was and continued to groan and cry till he died.

While they were thus occupied, the young man came to their dwelling, where he found a great quantity of bear's oil; and taking dry weeds, he put them in all the rooms in piles, poured the oil on them, and set fire to everything. Straightway the whole place was afire.

The women, seeing the destruction of their house, ran home and began to make water on the fire.

But in vain. Everything was burned. The walls fell in, and the house was destroyed except the outer entrance.

A great number of people had collected opposite on the lower bank, looking at the ruin of the house of these twelve women.

The little women stood on the edge of the cliff and, calling out to the people, said, "If you had left us in peace, we would have taught you many things, taught you to do what white-eyed people do who live over this great water here.

"A hundred years from now they will come here and drive you away, and you will have no land.

"You will be poor, no people.

"This is what will come to you for driving us away."

And they disappeared. And no one knows to what place they went.

JOHN ARMSTRONG, *New York*

The First Land Sale

Here's a version of the usual story in which an ancestral Delaware predicts the coming of strangers from across the water. Notice that this telling includes a riddle. The answer, evidently, is "a ship" (with its knifelike sail and cannon smoke rising from the deck). This version also includes a second prophecy, indicating that the Delaware, who have already been pushed halfway across North America, will eventually be forced into the Pacific Ocean.

The Delawares knew of the coming of the whites seven years before they came and were camped at the place, waiting for them to come. When they came, one of the Delawares could talk to them then: this was the man who, although he had never seen them, had sung about them seven years before. His song said:

> I saw somebody smoking.
> He had a knife in his hand.
> He was swimming on his back.

When the Delawares met the boat at the shore and took the whites up to their camp, the whites had lots of knives and dishes, hoes, axes, and so forth.

They showed the Indians these things, and one of the men stayed around and told people to come and look at their boat. So they went and looked at it.

There was a young girl in the crowd, and the white people caught her and took her away.

A year from then, the man returned with the girl, and she had one child. When he came, he brought more axes, hoes, knives, and plates and gave them to the Indians.

They did not know how to use them, but ran a string through the eyes of the axes and the other tools and hung them on their necks. Then the man told them how to use them. And then he told the people,

"I would like to buy a piece of land from you."

They asked him how much he wants for a very little patch. They won't sell it at first, but he says all he wants is as big as a "cow's skin."

The Indians said yes, "You can have that much," and they made the contract.

Then he began to cut the cowhide into a small string: I tell you, that string went around a hell of a big piece of ground. So he began to cheat the Indians first jump. And he's still doing it.

The whites will drive the Indians into the water before many years, I think.

ANONYMOUS, *Ontario?*

Why the World Doesn't End

One of the old prophecies states that when the Lenape have been pushed to the Pacific Ocean, the world will end in fire. Another says that the end will come when the turtle, who is always journeying westward, reaches the Pacific. Still another, more hopeful, allows that although an old woman is "weaving" the end of the world, her work, fortunately, is unraveled each night—some say by mice.

One time a man went to an old woman's house. She gave him food. He saw there was only a piece of corn. He thought to himself that this piece would not fill him up. He ate the piece of corn, and before he knew it, there was another to take its place. The man did this to each of the kinds of food. The old woman was over in the corner weaving a basket.

It is said that whenever the old woman finished the basket, the world would come to an end. This would never happen because each time, at the end of the day, the old woman had nearly finished the basket, but the next day she would find the mice had chewed and made a hole in it.

MARTHA ELLIS, *Oklahoma*

DOG STORIES

James C. Webber

JAMES C. WEBBER / 1881-1950. Called Witapanuxwe ("Walking with Daylight"), Webber was a well-known member of the Lenape community of Dewey, Oklahoma. Of Unami, Munsee, Cherokee, and African descent, he was a speaker of Unami and the authority for Frank G. Speck's often-quoted *Study of the Delaware Indian Big House Ceremony*. In Speck's words, Webber "typified Emerson's definition of a great man as one 'who in the crowd keeps the independence of solitude.' " (James C. Webber is the teller of "The Boy Who Had Dog Power," p. 113. Photograph by W. H. Holden, courtesy of the American Philosophical Society.)

The Wolves and the Dogs

In the old days dogs were a part of every family. At birth each child was given a pet dog, and it was said that if the child became sick, the dog itself would take the illness in order to spare the child. From archaeological evidence we know that people in the old Lenape homeland kept dogs as pets thousands of years ago. Here's a story that tells how the first dog came to live with the Delawares.

A long time ago when this world was new, wolves and dogs were friends. But now, at this time, everything is different.

Back then, when it got to be wintertime, the wolf said, "I am cold and hungry. Who is there who would go get a firebrand, so we could make a fire?"

The little mongrel dog said, "Oh, my friend, I will go get the firebrand."

The wolf said, "All right, so be it."

The little dog went to get the firebrand, saying, "We will soon have a good blazing fire, we will be warm." So he left, and he went to where the Delawares lived.

When he got near, suddenly a girl said, "Oh, there is someone who is very cute! I want to go see him. This is surely a little mutt!"

The girl began to pet the little mutt. She told him, "Come here, come here, you are cold. Soon I will feed you, I will give you meat and bread."

Oh, the little dog was happy, and he went into the bark house.

But he forgot to bring the firebrand.

Finally the wolf gave up, saying, "That old dog is a big liar. I'll knock him in the head if I ever see him."

For that reason wolves and dogs are afraid of each other to this day.

NORA THOMPSON DEAN, *Oklahoma*

The Boy Who Had Dog Power

By means of dreams or visions, young men and women used to acquire a guardian spirit to help them through the rest of their lives. The guardian might be a bear, a wolf —or, as this story tells, a dog.

There's a story about a boy and a dog left alone in a village—where the tribe had left them during a war with other tribes. It was in the days when roving bands moved from one location to another.

Sometimes these bands would leave people behind who were not able to go along for some reason or another. It happened in this case that the boy's parents had died, leaving him a sole survivor and only about fourteen or fifteen years of age.

He awoke one frosty fall morning with nothing to eat. For that matter, very often an elderly person who was feeble and sometimes sick and unable to go would be left in case of quick removal.

So this boy was left, and he went about the desolate village grounds and managed to pick up old bread and some bones left by the fleeing villagers.

So he came to one spot. He heard the cries of a little pup. So he listened, he located a little, poor, bony, flea-bitten puppy.

He was glad, overcome with joy. So he took charge of him, fed and cared for his little pup.

So he kept on hunting, caring for him, feeding the little dog.

By the fall, his dog had gotten to be a big dog and was a great aid to him in providing food for both.

So now the boy was studying about how to find the band who had left him homeless.

So one day the dog spoke to him. The dog told him, "Master, you've been kind to me and reared me to be able to help you. So now I make friends with you. We will be pals for a lifetime."

The dog told him, "You're thinking about going to your people, so I'm going to help you." They set out, the boy and his dog.

So the dog conferred power on him to turn into a dog, and gave him power to have the animals' instinct to know their home.

These two pals would travel together. At night they would locate game—deer, buffalo, and other game.

So wherever this boy went, the dog went along. By this time they had caught up with the boy's tribe.

So successful was the boy in killing plenty of game that the other young men began to guess about how he had gotten his skill.

So, finally, he brought in so much game that the other young men began to envy him.

And a good hunter those days was always in demand. He became popular with the women.

More and more he was closely watched.

So the younger set began to plan to beat him somehow.

He oftentimes counseled with his dog friend. On every occasion the dog friend would bear him out in his struggles against his enemies.

So, he had so many offers to marry some of the most prominent girls in the country that they planned every way to get the best of him. So at last the other young men caught his pal the dog and killed him.

So at once he began to fall down on his hunting skill. So, he went down in pity and despair. The dog was his *witisa*—his friend.

That ends my story.

JAMES C. WEBBER, *Oklahoma*

Why Dogs Sniff Each Other

Versions of this unusual story have been noted among the Creek and the Koasati of the southeastern United States. The tale is similar to an old European story type known to folklorists as "Why Dogs Sniff at One Another" or "Why Dogs Look at One Another Under the Tail"—a variant of which is told by the modern Maya of Guatemala.

There is another story about dogs, but I don't know if I should tell it. Maybe for children's ears it wouldn't sound so good.

[LISTENER INTERRUPTS:] "But you heard it as a child."

Yes, they told the same story to me as a child. You know, you see dogs, they smell each other when they meet. Well, they're looking for something.

■ ■ ■

Once there was a group of dogs—they were all related to wolves at one time. The dogs all lived together, and one day they sent one of the dogs after some firewood. They were getting very cold.

Well, this dog went to the camp of the Delawares to steal fire sticks, but the people become very fond of him and started to pet him and feed him.

Well, he just decided to stay with the people and

not take the firewood back. Meantime the wolves and dogs waited and waited, and he did not ever show up with the fire sticks. Finally they realized he'd just forsaken the dogs and wolves. And then after a while, they separated—the dogs and the wolves—because this dog lied to the wolves, and they became enemies.

So they called a council one day, the dogs did, and said, "We will hold this council to see what we can do about the wolves; they fight us every time they see us. So since our council house is clean and holy, we can't bring anything unclean into the council house. From now on, all of you dogs must detach your *kekunëmëwoo* and put them into the basket by the door."

So they all did. They threw them into the basket and went into the council house and took their seats.

Now the long dog, we call him *chëmingw*, a long dog with a long shape—he's said to be the smartest of all dogdom—he made his opening remarks. He stood up on his hind legs and said, "Well, *mwekanewtuk*"—that means fellow dogs—"I want to hear from each of you. What have you to say about the wolves?"

When he closed his speech he sat back down and the other dogs got up from time to time and made their remarks.

Then, during one of the speeches, a huge wolf stuck his head in at the door of the council house. The dogs became so frightened that they all ran out of the council house, knocking each other down as they bumped into each other. The whole place was in confusion as they all tried to squeeze out of the doorway.

Now, as they went by the basket, each one tried to grab his own *kekunëmëwoo*. But because of the confusion each one took the first one he could grab. As they ran off into the woods they put these back on, but it was pretty certain that some of the dogs had gotten the wrong one.

That's why, to this day, the dogs are still looking around for their own *kekunëmëwoo*. Old people insist that it's the reason dogs smell each other. Each one thinks the other may have his *kekunëmëwoo*.

NORA THOMPSON DEAN, *Oklahoma*

How a Dog Earned the Right to Eat from the Table

Well known as a Delaware storyteller, the late Nora Thompson Dean was also the founder of a mail-order service, specializing in Delaware crafts and books. At the end of each year she would send her customers a greeting in the form of a short story in Delaware and in English—a custom that has been continued by her family since her death, in 1984. The following is one of her greeting stories.

A long time ago there was a man who lived in a big forest. He lived alone, except for his dog.

On many evenings they would talk together, this man and his dog. Then one day the dog said, "All right, my friend, let's go hunting! It seems like I can smell many squirrels toward the north."

So they left to go squirrel hunting, this man and his friend.

While they were walking along a little path, the dog suddenly heard something making a rattling noise by the path. The dog said, "Stop! Stop! I hear something! It might be a rattlesnake rattling!"

Then the dog grabbed the snake and began to shake him. And he shook him until he had killed the snake.

Then, when they had finished hunting, they went home. The man began to cook. And he fed the dog on the ground.

But finally the dog wouldn't eat. He just had a scowl on his face.

The man told the dog, "What's wrong with you? Aren't you hungry?"

The dog replied, "Oh yes, I *am* hungry, but I want to know what the reason is that you feed me on the ground. Why cannot I also eat where you are eating?"

The man said, "Oh well, you can eat with me, you can come sit right here!"

The dog smiled. He began to eat. He was eating with his friend.

NORA THOMPSON DEAN, *Oklahoma*

Charles Elkhair

CHARLES ELKHAIR / 1848-1935. Called Kòkwëlëpuxwe ("One Who Walks Backward"), Elkhair was the most knowledgeable traditionalist of his generation and the last to be recognized as chief of the eastern Oklahoma Delawares. A resident of Copan, near Dewey, he was also a singer in the Big House and a leader in the Peyote Religion. (Charles Elkhair is the teller of the stories on p. 89. Photograph 1909 by M. R. Harrington, courtesy of the National Museum of the American Indian, Smithsonian Institution, neg. 2905.)

Glossary and Pronunciation Guide

In this book Delaware words are spelled according to the system used by James Rementer and the late Nora Thompson Dean (fully explained in Dean 1988-89, vol. 1). Briefly, unmarked vowels have the usual Spanish or Italian sounds *(ah, eh, ee, oh, oo)*; short vowels are marked *à* (as the *u* in *cup*), *è* (as in *met*), *ì* (as in *fit*), *ò* (as in *north*), and *ù* (as in *pull*); the vowel *ë* is like the *a* in *sofa*. Consonants are as in English, except that *x* has a throaty sound like the German *ch* in *ach;* and *th* is always two separate sounds, as in the English word *hothead*. Delaware words are ordinarily stressed on the next to last syllable; in exceptional cases the stressed vowel appears with an underline.

For most of the Delaware terms a very rough guide to pronunciation is suggested below, followed by "(U)" if the word is Unami Delaware, "(M)" if it is Munsee Delaware. One term, marked "(S)," is Seneca. All others are English.

band / a smaller group within the tribe; sometimes a lineage, or extended family group (p. 56).
chëmi̲ngw (ch-MINGW) (U) / dog with a long body (p. 117).

conjurer / probably the same as the "doctor," or medicine man, described by Heckewelder as one who is possessed of supernatural powers and who attempts to "counteract or destroy the enchantments of wizards or witches, and expel evil spirits" (p. 49). For Heckewelder, see References below.

dream helper / guardian spirit, source of personal power, typically an animal that has appeared in a dream or vision (p. 36).

fire drill / a fire kindling device in which a stick is revolved rapidly in a hole made in a piece of wood (p. 24, illustrated on p. xv).

flu! (U) / an expression roughly equivalent to the English "Shucks!" (p. 82).

ganyo gowa (S) / literally "great game," an animal thought to have special powers, believed to be a leader of other animals (pp. 68, 74).

kahamakun (kah-hah-MAH-kun) (U) / sweetened, pounded parched corn (p. 19, 20).

kekunëmëwoo (kay-koo-nuh-muh-WO-o) (U) / genitals (pp. 117, 118).

Lenape / English form of the word *lënape* (luh-NAH-pay) (U) or *lënapew* (luh-NAH-pay-wh) (M); Delaware, member of the Delaware tribe; literally, "ordinary person" or "real person" (pp. 75, 85, 86).

manëtu (mah-NUT-too) (U) / spirit, spirit power, supernatural; popularly "manitou," an English word derived from the Delaware (pp. 25, 75).

mwekanewtuk (mway-kah-NAY-wtook) (U) / fellow dogs (p. 117).

Nanticoke / a tribe formerly of Maryland, associated with the Delaware during their westward migration; or a member of the Nanticoke tribe (p. 23).

netyogwesûk (M) / (unusual spelling follows the source); perhaps an error for "ketyogwesûk," better written "kitshoxkwèshàk," little old women (pp. 99, 101).

puchël (POO-chul) (U) / messenger for a chief (pp. 50, 51).

Shawnee / a tribe now in Oklahoma, formerly of the eastern United States, historically associated with the Lenape (p. 33).

wampum / cylindrical beads made of white or purple shells, used as jewelry or as money (pp. 49, 51).

White River / a tributary of the Wabash, originating in east central Indiana (p. 23).

whoop / according to Heckewelder a yell consisting of "the sounds *aw* and *oh*, successively uttered, the last more accented and sounded higher than the first" (pp. 20, 40, 42, 62, 92). For Heckewelder, see References below.

witisa (wee-TEE-sah) (U) / his friend (p. 115).

yakwahe (YAH-kwah-hey) (U) / probably borrowed from Seneca *nyakwaehe:h* (NYAHK-wy-hey), i.e., the great naked bear, a mythical hairless bear dangerous to humans (pp. 62, 64-66). In the story the word is often capitalized and treated as a proper name.

Notes

Works referred to by author and date or by author only will be found fully listed in the References.

Introduction

Page 2 / Monmouth County: Revey, pp. 81-82. *Page* 3 / Ancestry of Nora Thompson Dean: Rementer 1990-93 (letters dated 8 Oct. '90 and 8 Nov. '93). *Page* 3 / Ancestry of Josiah Montour: Speck 1945, p. 2, and Goddard 1978, p. 237. *Page* 4 / "I'm very happy to be able . . . ": Dean 1976 (side A). *Page* 5 / Peter Lindeström: Lindeström, p. 208. *Page* 5 / Trowbridge: in Weslager 1972, p. 476. *Page* 7 / Stories published by Delaware Tribe: Hale 1984 and Hale 1984a. *Page* 7/ Close study of 220 stories: Bierhorst, forthcoming. *Page* 7 / "The earth is flat . . . ": Harrington 1907-10, Box OC-163, folder 9, no. 20. *Page* 10 / "One who mixes" . . . "one who feeds": Frank Speck in War Eagle 1929-45, p. 111; Nora Thompson Dean in Rementer 1990-93 (letter dated 8 Nov. '93). *Page* 10 / Bugs and worms: Newcomb, pp. 72-73. *Page* 10 / Snakes and lizards: Weslager 1978, p. 112. *Page* 10 / "When things around cannot hear": Harrington 1907-10, Box OC-163, folder 9, no. 21. *Page* 11 / Skunk skins: Dean 1977 (side A). *Page*

11 / Winter stories and summer stories: Dean 1978, p. 12, and Blalock in Rementer 1990-93 (letter dated 15 Mar. '91). *Page* 11 / Storyteller's bag: Harrington 1963, pp. 302-3, and Dean 1977 (side A). *Page* 12 / Pick up a stick and snap it across his knee: "Willie's Tales," *Time*, 7 Aug. '39, p. 45; and Voegelin 1945, pp. 108 and 110. *Page* 14 / "Dense woods": War Eagle 1929-45, p. 60.

Stories

Page 17 / How the First Stories Came Out of the Earth: Harrington 1907-10, Box OC-160, folder 1.

A version freely retold by Harrington appears in Harrington 1963, p. 287. The story is presumably from an Oklahoma source and therefore assignable to the Unami. Harrington, whose manuscripts are not carefully labeled, worked among the Munsee of Ontario as well as the (mostly) Unami of Oklahoma. The Munsee stories are labeled "Muncey" or "Minsi." The rest, unlabeled, appear to be Unami.

Page 18 / Snow Boy: Harrington 1907-10, Box OC-163, folder 9.

Other Lenape stories on the subject of winter include the cannibal tale (Voegelin 1945, pp. 106-10) and the story of how corn appeared (Gilliland).

Page 20 / The Giant Squirrel: Dean 1977 (side B).

Nicholas Shoumatoff, founder of the Delaware Resource Center at Cross River, New York, elicited this story and asked the question heard near the end.

Page 22 / How the Big House Got Started: Pearson 1969.

This and the two Wehixamukes stories on pp. 82-89 are preserved in Unami Delaware text with interlinear English glosses by Pearson. The glosses are here given in a connected version.

Page 29 / The Sun and the Corn Bread: Harrington 1907-10, Box OC-163, folder 9.

In the manuscript, Harrington prefaces the story with the annotation "Minsi / Sun, Ki'co, like a man, who travels all day across the heavens." According to a report of 1823 by C. C. Trowbridge, the sun—in Delaware belief—formerly devoured twelve children each day at noon "as a kind of compensation for his labors," but in response to human protests he now eats only two (Weslager 1972, p. 491).

Page 30 / The Boy Who Became a Flock of Quail: Montour.

Other Delaware story-songs—one about a troublesome mother-in-law, another about a boy who went squirrel hunting—are in Adams, pp. 124-25.

Page 32 / The Lost Boy: Harrington 1907-10, Box OC-161, folder 1.

The Delaware water monster, or "mermaid," here appears in a romantic guise. Better known is the tale in which the monster literally destroys people (see "The Big Fish and the Sun," p. 47, with note below).

Page 34 / The Girl Who Joined the Thunders: Harrington 1907-10, Box OC-161, folder 1.

Other Delaware stories about humans who joined the thunders are in Curtin 1923, pp. 206-10, and Newcomb, pp. 73 and 74.

Page 38 / Rock-shut-up: Harrington 1907-10, Box OC-160, folder 1.

The real-life Rock-shut-up is discussed in Rementer 1990-93 (letter dated 11 May '90), where the name is spelled A-sun-Ke-pon.

Page 47 / The Big Fish and the Sun: Michelson, folder 6.

The Unami Delaware name for the water monster is *wewtunëwes*, "that which draws under" (Dean 1978, pp. 12-13).

Page 56 / Ball Player: Harrington 1907-10, Box OC-163, folder 9.

Storytellers are sometimes forgetful. It will be noticed (on p. 61) that there are two remaining boys, as there should be. But the original manuscript has "three remaining boys." The text, then, has been corrected. A version freely retold by Harrington—with the brothers plainly numbered—appears in Harrington 1963, pp. 290-97.

Page 67 / The White Deer: Curtin and Hewitt 1883-, Box 2, pp. 67-71 of booklet with cover sheet bearing the inscription "Armstrong" and "Nov. 1883."

A rewritten version appears as "a Delaware story" in Curtin 1923, pp. 156-59. A variant (with different details, not merely a rewriting of the same text) is published as a Seneca story in Curtin and Hewitt 1918, pp. 519-25. It may be argued whether the tale was originally Delaware or Seneca. The term *ganyo gowa*, applied to the white deer, is Seneca, meaning "great game." But the concept of the white deer as game master is attested for the Delaware: "The Indians [i.e., Delawares] call a white deer the king of the deer and believe that the rest flock about and follow him" (Zeisberger, p. 64).

Page 75 / Three Boys on a Vision Quest: Rementer 1990-93 (letter dated 11 May '90).

The Unami Delaware word for "correction" is *kwëtëlëtëwakàn*. Other corrections: "Don't crack nuts after nightfall," "If one dreams, he should not tell his dream until after he has eaten," "Do not let the snow see you eating or he will tell the winter spirit to make it colder" (Rementer 1990-93, letter dated 25 May '90).

Page 79 / Jack Babysits: Montour.

"Jack the Numskull" tales are well known in European folklore, and in such stories the trickster sometimes plays the "literal fool," misapplying ambiguous instructions. Since the Delaware trickster is also called Jack, and is also a "literal fool," it is possible that some of the Delaware material has been adapted from European sources. A variant of the story at hand has been reported for the Wyandot (Barbeau, no. 69), but neither it nor any other Delaware trickster story is known to have a direct European parallel. See Thompson 1919, pp. 416-26.

Page 81 / Crazy Jack Puts His Nose to the Ground: Voegelin, pp. 111-12.

The tale as given here has been excerpted from a cycle of several Wehixamukes, or "Jack," stories published by Voegelin in Unami Delaware text with a word-for-word English gloss. The present version has been adapted from Voegelin's gloss.

Despite Voegelin's information, obtained from Willie Longbone, the late Nora Thompson Dean said she had never heard any Lenape use "Jack" as a name for Wehixamukes (Rementer 1990-93, letter dated 8 Nov. '93).

Page 82 / Wehixamukes Story: Pearson 1969, pp. 12-19.

See note to "How the Big House Got Started," above.

Page 85 / More Wehixamukes: Pearson 1969, pp. 21-33.

See note to "How the Big House Got Started," above.

Page 89 / Six Stories About Wehixamukes: Michelson, folder 9.

The six episodes given here have been excerpted from a considerably longer Wehixamukes cycle, labeled "Story of Wehixamokas, the Delaware Sampson, possibly from [Silas] Longbone with comments at end by Silas [Longbone] and [Charles] Elkhair." Among the comments is this by Elkhair: "Wehixamukes was kind of a doctor, too. He'd heal people when they were sick. But he had to be told plainly. If you said, 'Father, take pity on my child,' he would take his ax and put it out of misery. But if you said, 'Take pity and *cure* him, he would do it.' "

Page 99 / The Twelve Little Women: Curtin and Hewitt 1883-, Box 5.

Unattributed in the manuscript, the story is presumably by John Armstrong, the only Munsee Delaware authority known to have been consulted by Curtin and Hewitt.

Page 104 / The First Land Sale: Harrington 1907-10, Box OC-161, folder 1.

The Delaware story about the land sale has been told since at least the late 1700s. Its most characteristic feature, the incident of the cowhide cut into string, probably derives from a European source. According to a well-known anecdote, to which Vergil alludes in the *Aeneid*, Book 1, line 368, Queen Dido of Carthage negotiated the purchase of as much land as a bull's hide would cover, then cut the hide into strips to make a rope that encompassed a large district. Variants of the tale are known from the Shawnee and the Wyandot (Bierhorst, forthcoming).

Page 106 / Why the World Doesn't End: Hale 1984a, pp. 6-7.

The prophecy of the world fire is in Peters; for the turtle prophecy, see Speck 1931 (pp. 106-9).

Page 111 / The Wolves and the Dogs: Rementer 1968-92. Told by Nora Thompson Dean, abridged by James Rementer.

Page 113 / The Boy Who Had Dog Power: War Eagle, pp. 85-87 (letter dated Jan. 1, 1939).

The story was written by James C. Webber (also called War Eagle) as a letter to Frank G. Speck, the anthropologist with whom he often worked. Evidently Speck had suggested the project, since Webber concludes by saying, "I hope you outlined something for me to do later."

The term "friend," used in the next-to-last line, probably means "helper," or "spiritual guardian"—as it does in other Delaware stories, including "The Big Fish and the Sun," where a boy hero refers to the sun as "my friend" (p. 52, above), and "Ball Player," where the whirlwind and various animals are "friends" (pp. 58 and 62).

Page 116 / Why Dogs Sniff Each Other: Dean 1978, pp. 11-12. By permission of the Archaeological Society of New Jersey.

For European variants, see Aarne and Thompson, types 200A (Why Dogs Look at One Another Under the Tail) and 200B (Why Dogs Sniff at One Another). For the Creek and the Koasati, see Rementer 1990-93 (letter dated 8 Nov. '93). The Maya variant is in Redfield, p. 256.

Page 118 / How a Dog Earned the Right to Eat from the Table: Rementer 1968-92. Previously published in Kraft and Kraft, p. 41.

References

Aarne, Antti, and Stith Thompson. *The Types of the Folktale*. 2d revision. Helsinki: Suomalainen Tiedeakatemia, 1973.

Adams, Robert H. *Songs of Our Grandfathers: Music of the Unami Delaware Indians*. Dewey, Okla.: Touching Leaves Indian Crafts, 1991.

Barbeau, Charles Marius. *Huron and Wyandot Mythology*. Canada, Department of Mines, Geological Survey, Memoir 80, Anthropological Series no. 11. Ottawa, 1915.

Bierhorst, John. Mythology of the Lenape: Guide and Texts. University of Arizona Press, forthcoming.

Cranor, Ruby. *Some Old Delaware Obituaries*. [Bartlesville, Okla., ca. 1990.]

Curtin, Jeremiah. *Seneca Indian Myths*. New York: E. P. Dutton, 1923. NOTE: Two of the myths are labeled "Delaware."

Curtin, Jeremiah, and J. N. B. Hewitt. Mss. 3860, 5 boxes: Seneca [and Delaware] myths. [1883-.] National Anthropological Archives, Smithsonian Institution, Washington, D.C.

———. "Seneca Fiction" (ed. Hewitt), *32nd Annual Report of the Bureau of American Ethnology, 1910-1911*, pp. 37-819. 1918. NOTE: Comparison with Curtin, *Seneca Indian Myths*, indicates that two of the stories, nos. 28 and 110, are Delaware, though they are not here identified as such.

Dean, Nora Thompson. "Delaware Indian Reminiscences," *Bulletin of the Archaeological Soc. of New Jersey* 35 (1978): 1-17.

———. *Lenape Language Lessons.* 2d ed. 2 vols. Dewey, Okla.: Touching Leaves Indian Crafts, 1988-89.

———. Place names, visions, stories. 1976. Interview with Nicholas Shoumatoff. Cassette tape, call no. 16 (cat. no. C-2 and/or L-15), Delaware Resource Center, Trailside Museum, Cross River, N.Y.

———. Stories in Lenape and English. Nov. 17, 1977. Interview with Nicholas Shoumatoff. Cassette tape, call no. 52a (cat. no. 2DE-18 and/or 2DE-21), Delaware Resource Center, Trailside Museum, Cross River, N.Y.

Gilliland, Lula Mae Gibson. Ms. 3873, notebook 3: This is the true religion of the Delawares. . . . National Anthropological Archives, Smithsonian Institution, Washington, D.C.

Goddard, Ives. "Delaware," *Handbook of North American Indians* (ed. William C. Sturtevant), vol. 15, pp. 213-39. Washington, D.C.: Smithsonian Institution, 1978.

Hale, Duane K., ed. *Cooley's Traditional Stories of the Delaware.* Anadarko, Okla.: Delaware Tribe of Western Oklahoma Press, 1984.

———, ed. *Turtle Tales: Oral Traditions of the Delaware Tribe of Western Oklahoma.* Anadarko, Okla.: Delaware Tribe of Western Oklahoma Press, 1984. Cited as Hale 1984a.

Harrington, M. R. *The Indians of New Jersey: Dickon Among the Lenapes.* New Brunswick, N.J.: Rutgers University Press, 1963 (originally *Dickon Among the Lenape Indians,* New York: Holt, Rinehart and Winston, 1938).

———. Papers, 1907-10. Box OC-160, folder 1; Box OC-161, folder 1; Box OC-163, folder 9. National Museum of the American Indian, Smithsonian Institution, New York.

Heckewelder, John. *History, Manners and Customs of the Indian Nations* . . . (ed. Rev. Wm. C. Reichel). Philadelphia: Historical Society of Pennsylvania, 1876 (originally published 1818).

Kraft, Herbert C., and John T. Kraft. *The Indians of Lenapehoking*. South Orange, N.J.: Seton Hall University Museum, 1985.

Lindeström, Peter. *Geographia Americae* (trans. Amandus Johnson). Philadelphia: Swedish Colonial Soc., 1925.

Michelson, Truman. Ms. 2776: Ethnological and Linguistic Field Notes from the Munsee in Kansas and the Delaware in Oklahoma. National Anthropological Archives, Smithsonian Institution, Washington, D.C.

Montour, Josiah. Texts. Cat. 1173. Manuscripts relating to the American Indian. American Philosophical Society, Philadelphia.

Newcomb, William W., Jr. *The Culture and Acculturation of the Delaware Indians.* Anthropological Papers, no. 10. Ann Arbor: University of Michigan, Museum of Anthropology, 1956.

Pearson, Bruce L. Notebook, Aug. 1969. Contains stories in Delaware told by Nora Thompson Dean, transcribed from an audio tape with interlinear English glosses. In the possession of B. Pearson, Dept. of English, University of South Carolina, Columbia.

Peters, Nick. Letters to Frank G. Speck, 1937-38. Cat. 898. Manuscripts relating to the American Indian. American Philosophical Society, Philadelphia.

Redfield, Robert. Notes on San Antonio Palopo. Microfilm Collection of Manuscripts on Cultural Anthropology, no. 4. 1945. Joseph Regenstein Library, University of Chicago.

Rementer, James A. Letters on Delaware folklore and other Delaware topics, 1990-93. Manuscripts relating to the American Indian. American Philosophical Society, Philadelphia.

———, ed. Christmas letters based on texts by Nora Thompson Dean, sent to friends and customers of Touching Leaves Indian Crafts, Dewey, Okla. 1968-92. Manuscripts relating to the American Indian. American Philosophical Society, Philadelphia.

Revey, James "Lone Bear." "The Delaware Indians in New Jersey, from Colonial Times to the Present," *The Lenape Indian: A Symposium* (ed. Herbert C. Kraft), pp. 72-82. South Orange, N.J.: Archaeological Research Center, Seton Hall University, 1984.

Speck, Frank G. *The Celestial Bear Comes Down to Earth.* Reading, Pa.: Reading Museum and Art Gallery, 1945.

———. *A Study of the Delaware Indian Big House Ceremony.* Harrisburg: Pennsylvania Historical Commission, 1931.

Thompson, Stith. *European Tales Among the North American Indians.* Colorado Springs: Colorado College, 1919.

Voegelin, Carl F. "Delaware Texts," *International Journal of American Linguistics* 11 (1945): 105-19.

War Eagle [better known as C. C. Webber, Charley Webber, James C. Webber, etc.]. Letters to Frank G. Speck [1929-45]. Cat. 932. Manuscripts relating to the American Indian. American Philosophical Society, Philadelphia.

Webber, James C. *See* War Eagle.

Weslager, C. A. *The Delaware Indians: A History.* New Brunswick, N.J.: Rutgers University Press, 1972.

———. *The Delaware Indian Westward Migration.* Wallingford, Pa.: Middle Atlantic Press, 1978.

Zeisberger, David. *David Zeisberger's History of the Northern American Indians* (ed. A. B. Hulbert and W. N. Schwarze). Ohio State Archaeological and Historical Soc., 1910.